BLURB

I'm a bodyguard. I walk softly and carry a big...stick.

Too bad I have no idea how to use it.

I know what you're thinking. How the hell do you end up a virgin when you live in a city known for easy access?

But my focus is protecting the women of New York...not fulfilling my every desire.

Then I meet her.

(Sin *is Book 1 of the Sin Duet. The conclusion will come in Book 2,* Sinful)

SIN

M. MALONE
NANA MALONE

MALONE² SQUARED

ALSO BY M. MALONE & NANA MALONE

- The Shameless Trilogy -

Shame (prequel)

Shameless / Shameful / UnAshamed

- The Force Duet -

Forcful (prequel)

Force / Enforce

- The Deep Duet -

In Deep (prequel)

Deep / Deeper

- The Sin Duet -

Beyond Sin (prequel)

Sin / Sinful

Sin © May 2018 M. Malone and Nana Malone

A MALONE SQUARED PUBLICATION

This book is a work of fiction. The names, characters, places, and incidents are products of the writer's imagination or have been used fictitiously and are not to be construed as real. Any resemblance to persons, living or dead, actual events, locales or organizations is entirely coincidental. All rights reserved.

No part of this book may be reproduced, scanned, or distributed in any manner whatsoever without written permission from the publisher except in the case of brief quotation embodied in critical articles and reviews. For information address: **MALONE SQUARED**, 340 S Lemon Ave #9016, Walnut , CA 91789

ALL RIGHTS RESERVED

Print ISBN: 978-1-946961-17-4

1

—————

Matthias

"BOLLOCKS! You can't for the life of you actually think that the DC Extended Universe movies are better than the Marvel Cinematic Universe movies. It's just not true."

Oskar Mueller shook his head. "Wait, DC... is that the one with Captain America?"

I groaned and threw my hands up. "Now you're just taking the piss, mate. It's as though you haven't been listening to a word I've said for all these years."

Oskar chuffed, his lips barely moving. That was his version of a chuckle. It was as if the show of emotion cost too much energy. "Nah, kid. I'm just fucking with you. I know that it's Superman that's DC. Of course, Captain America is Marvel. All those Avengers movies, those are Marvel. Superman is DC for sure."

I shook my head. "I can't even. I'm done with this conversation."

"Don't get your panties all in a twist. Oh sorry—knickers, right? That's what you Brits call them?"

I just shook my head. I wasn't going to let Oskar bait me. Although, that was the German's favorite pastime. It was as if he sought me out just to poke at me. For someone who seemed so serious all the time, Oskar was always there for a prank or to impart some dry wit.

I was actually grateful for it. Oskar helped me feel *normal*. If that was even a thing. Most of the other guys were a little *too* careful around me. Jonas stayed ever watchful. Ryan and Dylan were cool, if not a little distant, with me.

Rafe was the worst. Despite the air of 'cool, relaxed, and not giving a fuck,' Rafe was always on high alert around me. But those feelings were mutual. Ever since Rafe tried to kill us all a couple of years ago, I didn't trust him. It didn't matter if he was Lucia's brother and thought we were the enemy at the time. The guy made my skin itch.

Noah was different. He was... well, watchful. Considering Noah knew just how deadly I could be, I had always wondered how he could allow me around his family. But Noah had faith in me. He always had. And because of that faith, I worked hard at appearing normal. After all, I'd kept the monster at bay, hadn't I?

Oskar playfully shoved my shoulder and the monster inside me twitched, as if trying to awaken from a long nap. I quickly shut that shit down, secured the locks again, and placed that thing from *Alien* in front of it on guard duty. There was no way I was letting that guy out.

Not with my family. There'd been a time when even the slightest touch meant it was time for blood. *But you don't live like that anymore.* No. That had been a very long time ago. I was a different person now. This version of myself didn't slice and dice my family for an affectionate shove.

"I swear Nerd Boy, you get wound up over the slightest things. Let's both just agree that Wonder Woman is legitimately the hottest superhero we've ever seen."

I pondered this. "Look, Diana is gorgeous but Black Widow... How can you not love Black Widow?"

Oskar frowned. "Which one is that?"

I dropped my hands. "Jesus Christ, now I know you're a tosser."

And then Oskar grinned. A full smile. No wonder the women fell at his feet. Even I was temporarily stunned.

You could learn a thing or two from him. No. No, I couldn't. I wasn't interested in any of that. *Liar.*

There had been a time when I had thought maybe Lucia... She was sweet, innocent—just the kind of girl I should want to go after, if I wasn't tainted on the inside. But she'd been in love with Noah. Always Noah. So I'd shoved those feelings aside. Besides, it wasn't as if I knew what to do with any of that.

Most women weren't clamoring for a psychopathic former killer who liked to watch people bleed. Nope, that would make for one hell of a Tinder profile.

I started in on Oskar again just as the buzzer on my watch started to vibrate on my wrist. I had a series of alarms set just in case anyone tried to breach our security protocols. It wouldn't be the first time. Most of the alarms were harmless. Some hacker kid was poking around in the wrong corner of the Internet. But if the secondary alarms went off as well, I had trouble.

I was so good at schooling my expression that Oskar kept prodding me as if everything was perfectly fine. Little did he know that I was silently letting out a little piece of my monster, the protective side, the one ready to kill to protect the new family I had carved out for myself. That monster, that little sliver of the death that was inside me, was all I'd ever let out. The rest of it was too dangerous, too ugly. That monster would leave me alone without anyone.

I inclined my head. "I want to go and check on something."

Oskar nodded. "Yeah, you go ahead. I'm going to put on *Wonder Woman* again."

"You're seriously going to watch that without me?"

Oskar nodded and winked at me. "Yep, I swear, watching Gal Gadot wield the sword is almost as good as watching porn."

I wouldn't know. I appreciated the female form as much as the next guy, but watching porn—that took me back to a place I never wanted to go again. So it was best if I just didn't go near it.

All work and no play makes the monster hungry.

I swallowed hard and shoved the thought aside. I took a sharp turn at the living room, heading down the hallway toward my room when I saw Rafe coming down the hall from the other end from Noah's office. I couldn't help it. A part of me wanted to start a fight, to test my skills again against Rafe.

It was something that happened every single time I saw him. Like the fight-or-flight instinct flared, and I always chose fight. Things had gotten a little less tense with the two of us, but there was something about him. He always reminded me that I could die at any moment so I had to be ready... on the go.

Noah didn't give me the same feeling. Even though he and Rafe had both been killers for the same government organization that had trained me, Noah didn't trigger that instinct in me. But Rafe always did. *Maybe that's because the guy tried to kill you.*

Yeah, tried being the operative word.

Maybe, but that was supposed to be all water under the bridge now. Noah had brought Rafe in from the cold.

I met his gaze evenly as we brushed past each other in the hallway. Rafe gave me a nod but I barely acknowledged him.

The alarm on my wrist went off again. This time three buzzers. *Shit.* Someone was really trying a breach. We were fucked.

As soon as I passed Rafe, I jogged down to my room and went straight for my monitors.

My room pretty much made up the entire center of the penthouse. It was the largest one in the penthouse but by necessity. I'd insisted that I needed to be close to the monitors just in case anything happened. I had servers in here, hard drives that needed to be destroyed and wiped if they were breached.

Maybe you wouldn't have so much trouble if you weren't starting a war. Sometimes a war was necessary. I put on my earphones and quickly pulled up the monitors, checking to see where the intruders were.

Fuck a tit. Personnel files. This wasn't the first time in the last several months that someone had tried to get access to who we had on our team. The Blake Security team information was public knowledge. Well, mostly public. Everyone's backgrounds were so scrubbed and embellished by me that the people we described were hardly recognizable. But still someone wanted in. And so I desperately needed to keep them the fuck out.

My fingers flew over the keyboard as I fought the distributed denial-of-service attack. Fingers flew over keys from one keyboard to another. I knew who was doing this. I'd been warned.

I managed to shut down one attack. The other one was nearly close enough to penetrate employee records. *Shit.*

And then I had it. With swift keystrokes, I'd stopped the attack.

Bugger, that was a close one. The signature was familiar though. Something tickled at my memory as if I should know this hacker's style... as if I should recognize it. As if it were me. The style was so similar to mine. I would have almost thought I was hacking myself.

Had the Family managed to get someone nearly as good as I was? Hell, maybe even better?

I didn't get to dwell on that question though because Noah popped his head in. "Hey kid, everything okay?"

I was used to schooling my expressions. It was really easy when most of the time I didn't have any emotions. "Yeah, fine."

Noah studied my face. "Are you sure? Rafe said you looked... off."

"I'm cool. I was running a diagnostics scan and my alarm went off letting me know that it was done. So I just came in here to check."

Noah nodded. He looked like he believed me, but some emotional responses escaped me as I was so used to shutting people out, shutting down their emotional input. I just didn't always know when to turn it on.

Noah was almost always easy. I knew my mentor's 'We have trouble' face. I knew the 'Get the fuck out so I can fuck my wife' face. I knew the 'Isn't my baby gorgeous?' face. I knew the 'Let's get down to business' face.

Everything else was nuanced and in-between and so much harder to read. But for the most part, Noah was wide open. Rafe, on the other hand, was completely impossible to read. The others were easy. The women? Jesus! JJ and Lucia—I never understood what the hell was going on with them. Diana was a little easier. She tended to have an 'Ask Kiki' face. So I was down with that one.

I knew Noah was assessing me for a lie. But I also knew that Noah wouldn't find one. The guy had trained me. I hated lying to him. After all, he'd saved me. But sometimes it was necessary.

When Noah left ORUS years ago, he'd made sure I could go with him. He had legitimately saved my life. He'd been clear that he wouldn't be leaving ORUS without me, and Noah had gotten me out not a moment too soon. One more day with that shadowy organization and that monster would have taken over my life... entirely. There would have been nothing left of myself.

"Okay, if you're sure. The whole family is in the living room. We're going to watch *Wonder Woman*. Oskar insisted. Are you coming?"

I gave a nod. "Yeah, I'll be there in a minute."

Noah hesitated. "Listen, kid. I know you've been under some pressure with Rafe back. But you know that you can talk to me about anything, right?"

Oh yeah? Like how I think about all the ways to kill your brother-in-law on a daily basis? Like that? I kept that thought to myself though. Normal people didn't think about killing people. That was the problem. At the core of it, I was a killer. Noah wasn't. Noah had killed. He'd been an assassin just like me. The problem was, I *liked* it. And that made me the boogeyman.

But you don't do that anymore. No. No I didn't. That was the reason for my locked up monster, after all. Now, the things I cared about were protecting my new family and taking down my old one.

My old "family" had sold me to ORUS like I was nothing... like I wasn't worthy of living. They had taken the only person I'd ever cared about in my life and killed her. And then they'd sold me off. So my slow, deliberate dismantling of their empire? That was payback.

And what if that payback blows back on your new family? The family I'd carved out for myself. The family I fought to protect.

I never thought of myself as capable of love. Maybe at one time I had been. But that love had died with that girl. I might not be capable of that emotion, but I felt strong affection and a need to protect my family. They were everything to me.

My watch buzzed again and I groaned, turning my attention back to the monitors. This time, it wasn't an attack. It was a message written in one line of code in my command window.

We're coming.

Well, they were welcome to come. I would kill them

all before I let any of that filth touch anyone I cared about. They were all going to die.

———

Gemma

I ADJUSTED my sunglasses on my face. I knew exactly where the cameras were, and I managed to avoid the majority of them. The ones in the luggage area were the more difficult to avoid.

But I knew the rules. Stay hidden and stay alive.

JFK was as busy as usual, a horde of people easy enough to get lost in. Once I had my bag, I deliberately separated myself from the throng and then made my way to the ladies' room. After waiting in line for nearly thirty minutes, I bounded into a stall, changed my clothes, and dragged off the blond wig I'd been wearing before shaking out my dark locks.

After I was done, I studied myself in the mirror. Anyone looking for me would completely miss me. I'd traded the wig for my natural hair. Well, my naturally *dyed* hair. My natural color? Red. When was the last time I'd seen that?

I missed it sometimes, but while I was undercover with the Family, black was better. They might have recognized me as a redhead. Maybe not, but better safe than sorry.

I picked up my rental car and tossed my roll along bag into the trunk. The moment I was in the driver's seat, I took out my phone and made a call. "I'm in."

The voice on the other end of the line was terse. "You understand what you need to do."

"Yes, I understand. When will I get the target?"

"We'll give you the target when you're all settled. We don't want you getting all excited now. There's a plan in motion."

I was already regretting this. When I'd been asked by the government organization that I worked for, ORUS, to go back undercover in the one place I'd vowed I would never return, my answer had been an all-encompassing "Fuck, no."

But they dangled the carrot of all carrots: *revenge.* And now I was a double agent. Every day was a big game of Russian roulette with my life. *Oh the good times.* But if I wanted access to the head of the criminal organization known only as the Family, then I was going to have to complete their stupid initiation rite. *Stupid or not, it means killing someone. Are you ready for that?*

As an ORUS agent, this wasn't my first kill. But it was the first kill where I knew nothing about the target. ORUS targets were sanctioned by the US government.

They took out the worst of the worst. Scum of the earth. ORUS was the cleanup crew.

I didn't know who the hell the Family was sending me after. Although, whoever it was, if they had an association with the Family, it meant they weren't clean. *But still, can you know that for sure?*

I shoved that thought out of my head.

"Of course I want everything that you're offering, but to be successful at my job I do need some information."

"Ah, Avery, you're always so intent on doing a good job. Not to worry love; you'll get to meet Father. You'll get what you've been looking for this whole time; to become a fully pledged member of the Family. You just have to carry out this one last job."

I knew what *wasn't* being said. If I didn't do what I was told, they were going to hurt my friend.

I'd known better. Befriending people in the Family could get you killed. But the moment I'd been back undercover, I'd seen her. I remembered her from before when I was a child. And I hadn't been able to shut her out.

But of course, those wankers had seen my soft spot for the kid. So to make sure I carried out my job, they'd taken Sabine away to a *safe* location. Somehow, I was sure Sabine was anything but safe. But they'd taken her to ensure I was serious about becoming a member of the Family.

Sabine worked as a drug mule for them. She hadn't been sold into prostitution yet, but I was terrified that was what was going to happen to her. The guilt from leaving her behind that first time ate at me.

I needed to do this job, get to Father, and get Sabine the hell out of there. Thanks to my job at ORUS, I had money, plenty of it. I could give it to Sabine to start a whole new life, but first, I had to do this. And if my target was innocent I had to find a way to save them too. Easy as pie. *This is the job. Too late to back out now.*

"I'll do what you say. I'll be at the safe house."

After hanging up, I took the SIM chip out of the burner phone, slipping it back into the case into the little protector slot labeled A, for Avery. My code name with the Family.

Then I took out another SIM chip from the slot marked G. I grabbed my other burner phone and slid the chip inside.

When I was abroad, this was how I kept my two mobiles separate. I found it funny how neither of my two cells were my original self.

A long, long time ago, my name had been Gigi, and I'd been a bright-eyed, red-headed girl full of hope and love. And then the Family had taken me.

I never thought I would know love or hope again, until I met Matt and he made it his life's mission to protect me. But, of course, his protection hadn't been enough. He'd nearly gotten us both killed.

So affection, it was a dangerous thing. I dialed the number I had committed to memory. After one ring, I hung up. Then dialed and let it ring for two rings, and hung up again. Finally, I sent a text and then called again. On that final call, the person on the other line answered immediately. "Persephone, status?"

"I've landed in New York. They still won't tell me who the target is. I'm supposed to go to the safe house and lie low, and then they'll give me instructions."

"You've got nothing to go on?"

I knew what my orders were from ORUS. I was to do whatever was necessary to gain the trust of the highest levels of the Family. If that meant taking out this target, then that's what I would do.

"I know nothing. All I know is that if I take care of the target, I'll meet Father."

"Whoever it is, they want him badly. So if they want him, *I* want him. It's risky, and we don't know where they may or may not have moles, but if we can take the target alive, talk to him, question him, that can be extremely useful to us. If need be, we'll tell the Family you had to put the target down. We'll fake proof of death."

"That *will* be risky, and there are other lives involved here."

He sighed. "I know you've made promises and we'll do our best to keep them, but that is not our primary objective. Do you understand?"

"Understood…" Except not understood. I was getting Sabine out of there whether Orion liked it or not.

I was playing a dangerous game. One that could get me and Sabine killed. Never mind whoever the hell my target was. I had to keep all three of us alive.

But I could do it. I had to do it. If I could get to Father, I could bring down the whole damn family: the people that destroyed my life; the people who took away the only other person besides my father that I'd loved. I was going to make them pay for everything, and I was going to stand back and watch them burn.

"My other mole inside the organization has no idea on the target either. But again, he is there to give us human trafficking routes and drug routes. Finding out about your target is above his pay grade."

I cursed softly. "I know. I'll call you as soon as I have more information."

Orion was silent for a beat. "Be careful. I understand

how great a risk this assignment is to you. Andromeda has already let me have an earful."

I let a smile tug at my lips. Andromeda had saved my life more times than I cared to count. She was still an active agent in ORUS, but I had a feeling that the woman would retire soon.

A long time ago, she'd pulled me out of the Thames, nearly drowned, sick, and had taken care of me, had given me a whole new life. I owed that woman everything. "Tell her she taught me how to take care of myself. I'll be fine."

"Get to the safe house, lie low, sunset the phone and the chip."

He always gave me the same set of instructions, as if I needed them. "I understand. Will do."

"Roger that."

2

Matthias

WHEN I WAS A BOY, I saw a fire break out in the council estate where I lived. I would never forget the terror on people's faces as they'd watched everything they owned burn right before their eyes. I'd been too young then to truly understand how far-reaching a disaster like that could be, but I'd understood all too well what it was like to have nothing.

I'd been an expert even at that young age.

Now, years later, I watched the lines of code streaming past on my screen and felt the same bone-deep emptiness I'd felt that day. I couldn't stop this attack. Blake Security was in chaos and there was nothing I could do.

Panic clawed at my throat as I continued to furiously type commands.

My mind racing, I tried everything I could think of. Then I tried things I was sure wouldn't work but I was desperate enough to try anyway. But no matter what I did, section after section of my network went down. It was like watching dominoes fall.

I wasn't being at all dramatic to say it was like watching my world come to an end.

"I've been shut out. I've been shut out of my own system."

The words hung in the air, sharp as knives. I was sure if I said them too many times they'd slice my lips to ribbons. But I had to do it. Saying it aloud made it all too real. It was just the slap in the face I needed to bring me out of the trance I'd been in since I'd first discovered the breach.

Like a shot, I was out of my seat. As soon as I hit the hallway, I called out, looking for my friends.

"Noah! Lucia!" I thought back to earlier tonight, trying to remember where everyone was going.

It was dark in some areas but the lights were still on in the kitchen. As if on cue, the lights went out, plunging me into darkness. We'd just discovered that we could control the lights remotely. I let out a disgusted sigh. There was no way of knowing just how much damage had been done so far by whoever was mucking around in my system.

"Help! Somebody help!"

I rushed forward at the panicked scream. It was a woman, which reawakened my fears that everyone hadn't left as planned. When I got closer to the elevator, I realized the sound was floating up from a floor below.

"Lucia?" I asked incredulously.

"Matthias! Thank God! We were on our way back up when the elevator stopped."

Noah spoke up then. "Matthias, what's happened?"

My boss's voice was steady but I'd known Noah a long time. This was his damage control, *don't-freak-out-Lucia* voice.

"There's been a cyberattack. I'm trying to get the cameras back online and restore my access but it might take a minute."

Before they could respond, I heard a pounding coming from behind me. I whirled around, drawing my weapon in one fluid motion. Panting, I glanced right and left, looking for intruders. Nothing.

Not wanting to give away my position if there was someone in the penthouse with me, I didn't bother to update Noah and Lucia on what I was doing. I could hear Noah still talking but I didn't turn back. At least if there was someone in the penthouse with me, they were safe in the elevator.

For now.

Although it would have been really fucking convenient to have Noah to back me up right about now.

I kept my eyes trained on my surroundings as I traced my steps back to my room. Whoever had gotten into the system hadn't turned off the power yet but it was only a matter of time before they figured out how to do it. If I had even a chance in hell of stopping them, I needed to regain control before that happened.

Just as I was sitting down, my phone rang. I snatched it out of my pocket and answered without even checking the number.

"What?"

"It's Dylan. Ryan just tried to log in to the system and he's getting an error."

"We've been hacked. Don't come back yet in case it's a trap." I hung up and immediately sent a text with the same message to everyone. Whoever was behind this had spectacular timing, locking down the system when Noah and Rafe wouldn't be able to help me. Lucky.

Unless it was planned that way.

Whoever had executed this plan was skilled. Very. I was one of the best hackers in the world and it wasn't false modesty that told me so, merely the number of systems I'd broken into over the years. It wasn't often I met a system I couldn't gain access to, and all of that experience breaking in places uninvited had given me unique insight on how to keep people out. So for someone to take control of a system I'd designed by brute force, it wasn't a garden-variety hacker. Maybe not even one person. In all likelihood, it had taken a team working on it together.

Which could mean that my past was coming back to haunt me. Finally. But if that was true and someone was coming to take me out, I'd go out in a blaze of glory.

Reaching under my desk, I unclipped the Glock that I always kept there. Next, I reached over to the shelf behind my desk and pulled forward my three volumes of the Lord of the Rings series and slid out the knives I kept hidden behind the books. Whoever was coming in, they'd better have done their homework. Because hacking was one thing; hand-to-hand was another.

At least I'd get to look the bastards in the eyes before I slit their throats. I was in the killing zone now. Nothing could bring me back.

Then I heard the one sound guaranteed to penetrate through to the heart. A baby's cry.

"Isabella. Oh bloody hell," I whispered. How could I have forgotten?

When Noah and Lucia had gone out for a quick bite, they'd only planned to be gone for an hour or two so they'd felt comfortable leaving the baby with me. Isabella slept so well that I rarely had to do much anyway when they left, other than the time I'd knocked her pacifier out and she'd screamed bloody murder until I'd found it and given it back.

I stood, my blood prickling in my veins like ice. This wasn't just about me anymore. Whoever had chosen tonight to attack had signed their own death warrant. Because I would die myself before I let any harm come to Izzy.

Gemma

WAITING in theory was much easier than in practice. I had given myself plenty of time, leaving my hotel room earlier, being sure to dress in jeans and a black, long-sleeved shirt—nothing that would attract undue attention. I'd taken a cab to the first address provided and then, per instructions, walked to the second address.

I stared up at the imposing glass and concrete structure, my burner phone clutched in my hand. This was the target? A security company? Knowing that my time was short, I whipped the T-shirt over my head to reveal the tight black compression vest beneath. This thing was designed to withstand a lot of force, was bullet-proof, fireproof and could even keep me afloat if I found myself in deep water. From my pocket, I pulled out a band and tied my hair back. I would put on a mask before going in and would need my hair to be out of the way.

This area of town was busy so I kept to the shadows, feigning interest in the screen of my phone. But while I waited, I used the time to scope out the building. There was only one entrance visible from this side. Honestly, it looked like a run-of-the-mill office building or maybe a warehouse of some type.

I wasn't sure what I'd been expecting but this wasn't it. Usually the Family had much loftier goals but perhaps this security company had information they needed.

Disgust roiled in my belly. God, I was tired of this. Living my life in the shadows, always at someone else's whim. I thought back to the long-ago night when my mentor had fished me from the icy waters of the Thames. The night I should have died but instead had been granted a new life. My mentor, Andromeda, had taken care of me, taught me to defend myself and trained me to be a weapon so I'd never again be vulnerable the way I'd been as a child. But I couldn't deny there were moments, in the dark of night, where I wondered if being saved that night was truly a mercy. Was this really a life I wanted to lead, being used to further the agenda of men drunk on the thought of more money and power?

Oh yes, even though I was undercover with the Family and had seen close up the atrocities they'd commit to solidify their power base, I was under no illusions that ORUS was much better. The organization had saved me, true, but it didn't mean I was blind to the things going on behind the scenes.

Even a broken clock was right twice a day. I shook my head at the thought. It had been something Andromeda used to say when I would question their methods or strategies. As a teenager, I'd accepted it as being an easy way to brush off my questions. But now that I had more experience under my belt, I wondered if my mentor hadn't been trying to justify the things they did in her own mind as well. If I was this conflicted about the ORUS mission after only seven years, I couldn't imagine the moral compromises one would have made after a lifetime in. Not that I knew Andromeda's age. Questions were one of the first things I'd learned to squelch. An inquisitive child, I'd quickly learned that people in my strange new world didn't take kindly to anyone trying to ferret out personal details.

Not even the ones who claimed to trust you.

Some life.

Whatever. Shaking my head, I pushed away the uncertainty. I was here to do a job, and Sabine's life depended on my succeeding. If this was the place I was designated to infiltrate, then so be it.

The phone in my hand vibrated. I raised it to my ear but did not speak, per my instructions.

You have three minutes to get up the stairwell to the penthouse level. The voice sounded robotic, like a computer.

I had so many questions. What if I took longer than three minutes? What if someone saw me? But instead, I waited quietly.

A second later, the robotic voice continued. *Once you reach the penthouse level, your target will be alone. You have seven minutes to secure the target and exit through the rear door.* The click in my ear was the only indication they'd hung up.

Well, that was that, then. I sighed. It was crazy to go through with this on so little information but what choice did I have, really? Bring back the target or my friend would die? It was an impossible choice.

Being an ORUS agent for the past decade had taught me plenty about impossible choices. And I didn't have the time to ruminate on my decision because I had no doubt the voice wasn't joking when it claimed I only had three minutes to get upstairs.

Tucking the phone into my vest, I walked quickly to the east side door, letting out my breath when it opened easily beneath my hands. The stairwell was dark as I sprinted up the floors, barely breaking a sweat as I passed floor five, six, seven and on.

At the top level, I paused briefly to allow my heart rate to settle and patted the Sig Sauer at my hip. More than likely I wouldn't need the weapons I'd been issued, and it was a definite that ORUS would prefer I didn't use them. Whoever this target was, Orion wanted him alive and well when I delivered him. No matter. It should be easy work to incapacitate some middle-aged office worker. I glanced down the stairwell I'd just ascended as it occurred to me I'd have to take him back down the same way I'd come up.

Change of plans.

There was no way I'd be able to get in, subdue the target and then carry him all the way down. He'd have to be conscious so he could walk down the stairs on his own. Otherwise, it would take too long.

Seven minutes.

The echo of that robotic voice urged me forward. I was wasting time.

The click of the door sounded loud in my ears as I entered the penthouse level. A baby's cry in the distance stopped me in my tracks. What the bloody hell? There hadn't been anything in the briefing about a child.

Motion up ahead caught my eye and I shrank back against the wall. If there were a baby here, I might have to take care of more than just the target. My eyes closed briefly before I blocked out all emotion as I'd been taught.

It was time to take care of this.

3

———

Matthias

Fuck.

Fuckity fuck.

Fuck queen and country. Fuck a duck.

The alarms were still blaring. The watch on my wrist vibrated over and over again, and I was helpless to stop the cyberattack that was happening.

And Isabella was still crying.

Multiple denial-of-service code attacks were happening at once and I wasn't fast enough to kill them all. It was as if whoever had tried to break in before had learned their lesson and had come back with multiple friends who were pissed off because I'd insulted their mother, or in this case, their father.

I shut down one attack, only to have another one pop up on another server. I rolled my seat around backward and forward, killing off attempts to hack into my system. All around me alarms blared when the cameras went down. *Jesus Christ.* I'd poked a hornet's nest all right. The power went out and the generators went on. But even though the generators had come on, an alarm went off in the elevator, which meant it was still stuck.

Fuck me. *Stay calm. Deal with one problem at a time. That's all you have to do… one step at a time.*

My phone rang and kept ringing. Noah. I put it on speaker. "I'm a little busy right now."

"Yeah, I figured, considering that Lucia and I are still stuck in the elevator."

And then all the alarms flashed red on my monitor, letting me know that all exterior doors were locked and interior ones too. *Shit.* That meant that anyone in the conference room, the gym, and maybe the bedrooms was going to be locked in for the time being. *Fuck. Fuck. Fuck.*

"Everything okay? How serious is it?"

Do not tell him. You can handle this. "I'm working on it. I've got it handled."

"It's fine. I just want to make sure Izzy's okay."

"I'll bring her in here with me while I'm working on this. She'll be fine. I'll find Rafe, too. I know he's around here somewhere."

Noah was silent for a moment. "Matthias, what the fuck is going on, kid?"

"Not the time for questions Noah. I'll get Izzy." I hung up on my mentor, knowing that I'd probably pay the price for that one later. But right now, I had other fish to fry.

I pushed up out of my chair, and then jogged out of my room to Izzy's. The generators powered the lights lining the hallways, so at least I wasn't running in the dark. As I approached Izzy's bedroom, the screeching got louder. My heart hammered as I leaned over and scooped up the baby.

"Hey, love. That's a good darling. That's a good girl. Uncle Matthias is here. No need to cry."

She blinked teary gray eyes up at me, and then a chubby hand reached up to smack my face. "Baba?"

It was as if she was asking me where her papa was. Fuck, I didn't speak baby. "Your mum and dad are coming, I promise. You just have to stay nice and calm for Uncle Matthias, okay? We had a little emergency." I kept my voice calm and cooing, and it seemed to do the trick because the tears cleared quickly and she started to coo and giggle at me, clapping her hands and starting to point at things. She was just on the cusp of talking.

"Mata," she babbled and patted me on the cheek then proceeded to babble a string of nonsensical words.

I could only imagine what that was going to be like in the future. She would probably go nonstop. Between the baby and JJ, I might need to find some earplugs. I found her little walking-stroller-type thing, the one with all the bells on top of it, settled her inside and strapped her in.

It looked like a stroller, but this one encouraged her to keep walking, which was just fine by me because I needed her occupied while I dealt with whoever the hell was trying to break into my systems. When I pushed her into the hallway, I called out. "Rafe? Are you here? I need you to watch Izzy."

But there was no answer. I did a quick mental calculation on where everyone was supposed to be. Rafe was in the penthouse somewhere, which made it odd that he hadn't come to investigate what was going on yet. Noah and Lucia were in the elevator. Ryan was on a gig. Dylan had his day off. Jonas and JJ were on their honeymoon. The new recruit was on a training op with some friend of Noah's who ran a bodyguard agency, and Oskar was in the living room which was on lockdown. So everyone was accounted for. All I had to do was find Rafe and

Diana. But as soon as I walked down the hall toward the living room and past the gym on the left, I froze.

Well, you found him.

Rafe stared at him from the other side of the glass in the gym, hands on his hips looking pissed the hell off. Diana was lifting weights, as if the blaring alarms and the power going out hadn't impeded her desire for a workout.

Rafe motioned to the door, but I shook my head. With a series of pantomimes, I tried to explain to him that something had happened and our power was off ... that I couldn't open the doors until I got the system fixed. Rafe's gaze slid down to where Izzy was happily playing with the balls in front of her, and his lips set into a firm line.

I scowled at him. Did the bastard really think I couldn't look after the baby? The guy didn't look pleased that I was the one that was left with her. "Yeah, well, not my choice either." I cared about Isabella. She was innocent and deserved protection and love. I couldn't offer love, but protection... That was in my wheelhouse. I'd die before I let anything happen to the baby.

Isabella looked up and waved one of her balls around, tossing it at me. I caught it then gently let it come back to her in its tether. She giggled then threw one to her uncle. When Rafe didn't catch that one (because, hello, barrier), Izzy scrunched her face. I knew right away that there were going to be tears, and I bent down. "No, no, no, no. Listen to Uncle Matthias's voice. You're fine. Look, I got your ball for you. No need to cry."

The last thing I wanted was a crying baby on top of all the noise and the alarm going off on my wrist again. God damn it. I needed to get back into the room. Well, Rafe wasn't available, so Izzy would have to come with me. I just hoped she didn't touch anything. The walker would only keep her occupied for so long.

I glanced back up at Rafe and tried a pantomime that I was going to take the baby and go back to my room to try and fix what was going on. Rafe frowned for a moment as if not understanding, then nodded. Isabella waved to her uncle and patted one of her chubby hands on the glass. Rafe bent down on his haunches and put his hand up too.

Rafe's hand was huge, much larger than Izzy's head even. She looked as if she was trying to measure her palm against his. Rafe seemed to say something to her, but no sound came out because the glass in the gym was soundproof. When Rafe stood, he nodded at me as if to say, 'Go do your thing, kid.'

I took hold of the handle at the back of the walker. "Okay princess, I'm going to see if I can fix this mess and get your mummy and daddy out. Whoever is doing this are a bunch of meanies."

Izzy answered by blowing a raspberry.

Her full cheeks and bright eyes had a smile tugging at the corner of my lips. "Yeah, sometimes I feel that way about people too." Just as I turned to push her back toward the bedroom and my monitors, I saw a shadow behind me. Immediately, I whipped around and shoved Isabella's walker so she rolled forward into the darker corner next to the gym.

I caught Rafe's look of horror as I was turning, and then I saw that I hadn't been imagining it. That was no shadow. Once again, the penthouse had been breached.

Gemma

HEAT AND ADRENALINE flooded my veins. This had to be him.

The target.

Jesus Christ, what was he doing with a child? No one had said anything about a kid. To my right, I saw a man and woman in the gym. The guy was tall. Huge really. And even through the glass, I could feel the fury directed at me. But he didn't come for me, which meant he was locked in.

I'd been told that someone would take care of the security system and it looked like it had happened. So the Family had done their part. And now I had to do mine.

In the corner, the baby cried and tossed out a ball. *Shit.* I didn't want to scare a baby. This didn't fit what I'd been told. *Get your head in the game. Otherwise you're going to die.*

I drew my baton and stepped forward. Never mind the fear or the sheer terror of facing off against this guy; I had a job to do. Problem was I had a distinct impression that this was my funeral and I just didn't know it yet.

With a deep breath I sprang into action, wielding the baton over my head. He stopped that attack easily by reaching up and grabbing the baton, and then delivering a punch to the gut that winded me, but I was ready for him.

While he'd been busy blocking, I'd taken out my knife and sliced across his abdomen. A long time ago, Matt had taught me the importance of always having a knife on me. But instead of crying out like I expected, all he did was hiss. Almost as if the kiss of my knife was a caress.

Problem was, with a slice like that, I hadn't cut deep enough. Because I wasn't actually trying to kill him. *He doesn't know that.*

He had my hand and he wrenched it just hard enough for me to drop my knife. And when I did, he hit me in the face.

I tasted blood... so much blood... and pain right behind my eyes. It wasn't the first time I'd been hit in the face, and it wouldn't be the last. I could survive it. It was more of the surprise than anything. When he lunged for me, I deftly blocked the next blow and got in one of my own. Open palm to the nose. That time, he did grunt. But his hands were up and we were trading elbows. From the way he fought, I could see he was remarkably well trained.

As well, if not better than I had been. The way he moved, I could see the Krav Maga training, the jujitsu, and the Muay Thai. And he used the full range of his movement.

As weapons of choice, I didn't like elbows. It didn't bode well for me. Even though I was tall, elbows required close combat. Up close and personal, and with this guy, the further away I stayed the better.

Why hadn't the Family warned me?

But as much distance as I tried to put between us and still deliver effective punches and kicks, he tried to keep me close. As if he knew that elbows and knees would end this fight if he could just land one on my temple.

With a swift uppercut, I managed to stagger him just a couple of inches and then I went for the kill and pulled him in for a knee. With my hand on his shoulder digging into his skin, my forearm across his trachea, and my other free hand positioning his arm out of the way, I delivered another crippling knee blow. That time he did groan, but he recovered quickly enough and head-butted me.

The clunk of our heads together had me seeing stars and I staggered backward. The target, though, he didn't stagger. He just kept coming for me, the menace and anger etched on his expressionless face. His eyes were cold, calculated.

As he approached, I delivered a roundhouse to his midsection, and he caught it, upending me and tossing me in the air.

Motherfucker.

I knew how to land though, arms splayed out to disperse the force of my descent. I sprouted right back up into position and so it went. Fists, and jabs, and grunts, and kicks, and knees... so many knees.

At one point, he picked me up and tossed me on the ground and then climbed on top of me, and he frowned as if something was off, something was bothering him. He raised his fist to lay it into my face. I put all of my force and energy into raising my hips high and proud and bucked him off. When he fell forward, I wedged a knee between us, and with all my force kicked him off, and then we were grappling on the ground, twisting and turning, a mass of limbs, and elbows, knees and head-butts.

At one point, I had my arm across his trachea again, and then he dug his hands into the cap of my mask and tugged my head back. He tossed me aside as if I weighed nothing.

Pain radiated through my back as I slammed on the ground, but I was on my feet again, going for him. *You have the training. Fight for this.*

His gaze slid to the baby in the corner who had started crying now, wailing. Screaming for someone called Baba. I didn't dare glance over but I could feel the malevolence from the couple in the gym. They wanted out. I knew they couldn't get out. Everything had been locked down. It was just the two of us. And I wished he would give up the fight already. But something told me that he was no ordinary man. No matter what, he would keep fighting.

He wasn't giving up and neither the fuck was I. After all the training I'd gone through with ORUS, after everything I'd seen in the Family, I wouldn't quit. One of us was going to die before I quit.

You can't kill him though; you need him alive. ORUS wants him alive.

Fuck ORUS. I wasn't going to die for them.

Yes, you will. You have your orders. And you are a soldier whether you like it or not.

I lost my footing and he caught me by the neck, his hands pressing in and squeezing tight, backing me up against the wall. I knew I only had mere seconds. As he pressed me into the wall, his eyes went flat and cold as he squeezed my neck. I raised my arm up above my head, twisted my body to the left and brought down my arm with all my might. When his hands came off my neck, I raised my elbow and delivered a sharp crack to his nose. He howled and I was on him.

I ran straight for him, lunged, and jumped, wrapping my legs around his waist and then digging my thumbs into his eye sockets and pressing hard. He yowled, flailing. I brought my hand back aiming to punch him in the throat, but then he managed to wrap a hand directly around my trachea and squeezed. I gasped and choked and loosened my legs. He planted me against the wall with that move.

Jesus Christ, he was going to rip my throat out. To counteract him, I delivered a front kick, at the same time twisting my body just in time to lever his arm off. The motion should have broken his hand, but he twisted away just in time. As if he'd been anticipating a move like that. But then, he twisted back, delivered a backhand, and then came at me with a right hook that rang my bell. And then he was on me, fists coming at me, blow after blow, after blow. Then he delivered an elbow to my ribs and couldn't help it. I cried out. "Oh my God."

Just before he would have landed a blow that would surely have knocked me out, his fist poised in the air to end the fight once and for all, he froze. "What? You're a bleeding *bird*?"

For a moment, he stood frozen, as if unsure of what to do. Unsure of what had just happened. I didn't waste any time. I leaned back, lifted my foot and delivered the perfect kick.

With enough force, a kick like that could sever the femoral artery. It might not be enough to put him out for good, but I needed to live to fight another day. His face went bright red, and I could see the fury coursing through his veins. He wanted to kill me.

Well, he wasn't going to get that chance. Not today. I'd have to come back with reinforcements, because right now, if I stayed, I wasn't going to live through the night.

When he finally sagged, I ran around him and he

almost had me, his fingertips just grazing the edge of my foot as I ran past him down the hall. I fled back to the right, past the kitchen, and out the side door I'd come in through.

That had been close... too close. Who the hell had trained that guy? And why did the Family want him?

4

———

Matthias

Shock still ricocheting through me, I stumbled after the dark-clad figure. But by the time I reached the door leading to the stairwell, the echoing sound of footsteps on the metal stairs told me what I already knew.

I was too late.

"Fucking hell." I fell back against the wall, gasping. My ribs would definitely tell the story by tomorrow. I expected to have some bruises. Even though the assailant had been no match for me, she'd still managed to get some licks in.

She. Guilt warred with practicality. I'd never hit a

woman. Protecting women was at the core of Blake Security's purpose. But that hadn't been just any woman. I snorted. As fucked up as I was, it was no wonder that the thought of a woman kicking my ass turned me on. But she'd been good. *Really* good.

The way she'd handled herself spoke of someone who was used to fighting and knew how to work her smaller size and agility. No doubt, this wasn't her first fight. I shook my head. Look at me; I clearly was hard up if the thought of encountering her again got me riled up. Maybe this was why they'd sent a woman, knowing that it would throw me off my game.

I couldn't allow my ingrained chivalry to get me killed. After all, a bullet from a woman would kill just as easily as one from a man.

Although she hadn't seemed too intent on killing me. Strange, that. If anything, she'd seemed just as shocked to see me.

In the background, Izzy's cry reached stratospheric levels. Doubling back, I ran for where I'd left her.

Izzy rocked back and forth in her walker, her face scrunched up. When she spotted me, she only cried harder. No doubt with the lights off, she couldn't tell who it was. I pulled out my cell phone and activated the flashlight, putting it on the floor so my hands were free.

"It's okay, little love. It's fine," I crooned to the baby as softly as possible, hoping to calm her a little.

Not that it worked. Little Izzy was just as pissed off about this situation as I was.

Suddenly all of the lights blazed on with a surge of power. Izzy stopped crying then, blinking at the light. I scooped her up and hugged her close. If the lights were back on, hopefully that meant whoever was messing around in the system had made a mistake and triggered one of my fail safes.

A moment later, I heard Lucia's voice. "Matthias!"

"Back here. I've got Izzy."

She burst into the room and let out a sigh of relief when she saw me holding the baby. After her daughter had been kidnapped recently, we were all on high alert for possible security risks or threats. Tonight had basically been Lucia's worst nightmare come to life.

My worst nightmare come to life.

"She's fine. No one got near Izzy."

Lucia took the baby from me carefully, rocking her daughter in her arms when she started fussing. "Are you okay? Why does this keep happening?"

"That's the million dollar question, isn't it?" Noah's deep voice interrupted. He gave me a look. "Rafe is in the air ducts. He sent me a text that he's stuck."

"Jesus. What a mess." Oskar's voice came from

behind Noah. "I was fucking locked in the living room and couldn't see shit."

Noah thrust his hands through his hair in frustration. "We need to regroup and assess the damage."

The earlier guilt started gnawing at my stomach again. "I don't know what happened, boss. But someone got into the system. I need to go see how bad it is."

Noah clapped me on the back. "Go. Do what you can. Do you need medical attention?"

I was already shaking my head before I even finished the sentence. "I'm fine. She was good. But not good enough."

"She?" He frowned. "They sent in a woman?" Noah's brow furrowed. "Interesting. I wonder if they thought she'd have an easier time getting Izzy to go with her quietly. Just like last time."

I considered it. The last kidnapping attempt, the culprit had initially used a woman to gain access to Isabella also. But this felt different. I thought back to how the woman moved. I'd bet money that she'd been ORUS trained. "It wasn't a civilian this time. She was ORUS, I'm sure of it. There's no mistaking the fighting style."

ORUS employed a unique blend of Krav Maga and Brazilian jujitsu when training to ensure their agents were not only strong and brutal but agile.

"Fuck. We need to get a handle on this situation. If Ian has authorized a mission to attack us, then we need to be prepared."

Oskar looked between us. "What does that mean? I thought Ian was on our side."

Noah laughed bitterly. "There's only one side when it comes to ORUS: the side that proves most advantageous. Which means—"

"That Ian has found something he needs more than our cooperation," I finished. "I don't think this is going to end well."

Noah let out a disgusted sigh. "When does it ever? Okay let's get our shit together and meet in the conference room. And somebody help Rafe out of the damn air duct!"

———

Gemma

GETTING BACK to the motel was going to be a bitch.

Hell, getting down all those stairs to the ground floor had been a bitch. The stairwell had been dark most of the way down but suddenly all the lights had come on just before I reached the ground floor, and I knew I was out of time. Whatever they'd done to get me access to the building must have worn off.

My time was up.

I shivered as I struggled to walk normally, looking left and right, hoping to see a cab. Who knew cabs were so rare when you actually needed them? I walked for two blocks and then paused on the corner to wait. It was agony standing there, trying to look as though I wasn't in pain the whole time. Luckily, I didn't think I had too many bruises on my face.

It wouldn't do to attract that kind of attention. People tended to remember those sorts of things and I had no doubt that someone would be asking questions soon.

A cab finally pulled over and I got in carefully. After giving the driver the address to the motel, I finally let out a sigh and thought about everything that had happened. By the time we reached the motel, I was pretty sure that I was going to be shipped home first thing in the morning.

Bloody hell, I thought. But it wasn't my fault. No one had told me that the target was so well trained. I'd only been told no one would stop me and that he'd be alone. I'd expected a middle-aged, balding, out-of-shape desk jockey.

After the cab dropped me off, I entered my motel

room and immediately grabbed the small ice bucket on the desk. The last thing I felt like doing was walking down the hallway looking for an ice machine, but with the way I felt, ice was a must.

Ten minutes later, I eased out of my vest and got my first look at the kaleidoscope of bruises on my torso.

With one hand, I scooped ice into a small plastic bag. Every movement was excruciating but I couldn't risk calling anyone to come help me.

I was on my own.

"What the hell was that?" I muttered aloud. The longer I thought about that clusterfuck of a mission, the angrier I got. All I'd been told was to obtain the target, make it look like a death, and then deliver him to ORUS. I'd assumed the target was a civilian.

No one had said that I'd be fighting another ORUS agent. Especially not one that was older and more experienced.

"Shit," I hissed as the ice bag made contact with my ribs. Bloody hell, every inch of me was going to be swollen by tomorrow.

Who the hell was that guy?

He'd moved like water, every limb so fluid that watching him fight had been like watching a dance. It would have been beautiful if the end result wasn't me being beat to shit. It had been too dark to see much of his face but he'd definitely been older. No one could fight like that without years of experience.

Worse, he'd been ready for me. Ready for a fight. Almost like he'd been tipped off. Had I been double-crossed?

Was Orion working some other agenda?

I stretched out on the bed, trying not to think about how many disgusting things I was lying on before picking up the burner phone. I raised it and dialed the number I'd been given to report back to Orion.

If my theory was correct, he'd already know that I'd failed.

"Are you en route?" Orion didn't bother with a greeting.

"No. I'm at the motel trying to figure out why no one bothered to tell me the target was an ORUS agent. I was lucky to get out of there alive."

A muttered string of curses on the other end of the line was the only thing that told me Orion was there. Silence hung in the air, rife with possibilities.

Finally he spoke. "I'd hoped for a different outcome, but apparently the element of surprise wasn't as much of an advantage as I'd hoped. What makes you think the target was ORUS trained?"

"Are you serious right now? I bloody fought him. I

should have known there was trouble when I was sent to a security firm."

There was a moment of silence on the other end. "Where did you say they sent you?"

"A place called Blake Security."

Silence. And then one shouted "FUCK!"

"What the fuck is going on? You could have warned me! I would have gone better prepared. Like, maybe with a rocket launcher." I shifted slightly to keep the phone between my shoulder and my ear. The new position sent a stab of pain through my middle so sharp I almost lost consciousness. "That guy was unreal. I've never seen anyone move so fast."

More calmly now, Orion asked, "What was his build?"

"Tall. Very tall. Lean but muscled. British."

"Son. Of. A. Bitch."

"Pardon me, sir, but what the fuck are you on about?"

"Perseus is a legend for a reason. I want that target more than ever now."

I almost stopped breathing. "Perseus. *The* Perseus?"

Orion made a noise that warned me to tread carefully. "The one and only."

"I'm lucky to be alive then," I muttered. If Orion was telling the truth, then it truly was amazing that he'd left me alive. Just like any organization, ORUS had its cliques, outcasts and celebrities. Even I knew the story of how Perseus had been liberated along with his mentor, Leo. Mainly because usually the only way to leave ORUS was in a body bag. My own mentor, Andromeda, had cautioned me not to get any bright ideas about getting out.

Joining ORUS was like being reborn. Once you were in, there was no way out of the life unless you died again.

Which made me suddenly even more curious about the man I'd fought tonight.

"You know the legend of Perseus. I want him back."

Easier said than done. "Look. Tonight was a bust, but I think I know another way in. Blake Security provides protection, but they have a whole section on their website dedicated to domestic violence. That's my in."

I held my breath and waited. Finally Orion spoke.

"You plan to pose as a victim?"

I could hear the skepticism in his voice. "By this time tomorrow, I'll be black and blue. The bruises will only make my story more believable. Once I'm in and they trust me, I'll have unrestrained access to the target."

"Do you think the Family will give you the additional time?"

It was something that I'd been worried about also.

What if they called me off and sent in someone else? This was more than just a job. I had to do this. More than just my ORUS career was on the line here. Sabine was counting on me.

I ignored the little part of me that was excited at the thought of meeting the famous Perseus in the flesh.

"Go. If the Family authorizes it, then proceed with our plan as usual. As long as you bring Perseus to us after you send them something to convince them that he's dead."

He hung up and I tossed the phone on the bed. It wouldn't be long before my contact in the Family was calling for an update so I put the SIM card in my other phone. Sure enough, that phone rang five minutes later.

"Status?"

"Not complete. Target was harder to kill than anticipated. I need more time."

"No more time. Mission objective has changed."

My heart sank. Were they pulling me off the job? If they sent someone else on this assignment then Sabine didn't have a chance. I couldn't give them any reason to decide that we were expendable.

"No, wait! I can do this. I already have a plan to get back in there."

At least after outlining the plan to Orion, I was

better prepared to explain it this time. However, my contact didn't seem too impressed either.

"Proceed. However, Father has authorized us to tell you the target is part of a rival organization. He is an enemy of the Family along with several others that are close to him."

"Do I have more than one target now?" My fingers tightened around the phone. If they asked me to take out multiple agents, this was going to be a problem. Orion had authorized me to go after the target because he needed him. If I was ordered to kill others, would he ask me to fake those missions, too? Or worse, kill them? I didn't kill innocents.

"No. Target has not changed. However, the Family needs you to deliver a message to the target. From the shadows comes the sun."

I repeated it to myself several times.

"You have one week," the robotic voice continued. "Or your mission is aborted."

"I understand," I responded. "One week and I'll send proof of death."

"Do not fail again." The line went dead.

I closed my eyes. After putting the phone down on the bed next to me, I allowed my head to fall back against the pillow. The events of the night had finally caught up to me and now that the adrenaline was wearing off, I felt like I'd been hit by a truck.

But the pain was going to keep my mind on the task at hand. Because I couldn't afford to be caught off-guard again. This was my last chance. Tomorrow, I would show up at Blake Security and pull off the acting job of my life.

I had to convince them to take me on as a client. Otherwise, I was just as dead as they were. The Family didn't tolerate loose ends. If I couldn't deliver, then I'd become just one more thread they planned to clip as they continued on their mission.

5

———————

Matthias

For the last twenty-four hours, I had been trying to figure out what the hell had happened. *You know what happened. Your past finally caught up to you. There's someone better, and they got in to your system.*

I shook my head to clear it and shored up all potential access points into the system again. Since yesterday, no more attacks, but I was ready... on edge. Everything that happened yesterday was my fault. I knew it. The guilt gnawed at me every time I looked at Isabella. Because I'd been hell-bent on revenge, someone had almost gotten her.

Yeah, but who? And how?

I was one hell of a hacker. There was a time when the name Matt would have someone shaking in their boots and doing whatever they could to protect themselves. *But you haven't been Matt in a long time. Maybe you're losing your edge.*

It was possible. When I'd been at my best it was when I'd been next to starving... desperate... in survival mode. No one was denying me food now. No one was trying to kill me. Maybe I had gone soft. Maybe someone had exploited that. But to come after Isabella, that made no sense. How would the Family even know about her? How would *Father* even know about her?

Father knows everything. I'd learned that the hard way a long time ago. That lesson had cost Gigi her life. And now my family was in danger.

But that was a lie. Father didn't know everything. Because for years, I'd been costing the Family money. Disrupting business.

I was all too familiar with the head of the Family. And since being sold into ORUS, I had tried several times to find out the guy's true identity. But to no avail. But likely the previous Orion had helped Father bury his identity. ORUS was one of the few organizations that had that kind of power.

I had only ever known him as Father. I'd only ever

seen him twice, maybe three times, in my whole time with the Family, and I'd been born into that world... the underground of the underground... the disenfranchised, the thugs, the criminals.

The Family ran the part of brassy, dingy London that nobody wanted anyone to see. *Yeah, well, not anymore.* I would do what I had to do to take them down. Even if that meant leaving my new home and the people I cared about. I would do anything to protect them. But I had to do this. I had to take the Family down because of the kind of people they were. But if that fight was going to touch my family, I would leave.

Surprisingly, that thought made my heart squeeze. I frowned at that.

"If you're frowning, we've got trouble."

I glanced up from my laptop to see Ryan Delaney walk in. Delaney was only a year or so older than me. But somehow, I always looked at him as the kid, the younger one. He and Dylan were the newest recruits that had passed all their certifications. But they were more legitimate recruits, the kind that had gone to Uni and served their country. That sort of thing.

Not the kind that were bought and sold like cattle. Not the kind that had spent a lifetime killing. Our newest recruit, Tyce, was still being tested out. Only time would tell if he would last here. He was still having some extensive training, so he'd missed out on all the fun and excitement of yesterday. He was due back in a couple of days.

I nodded at Ryan. "Just trying to make sure it doesn't happen again."

The guy studied me closely. "So you don't think it was a one-off? You think someone's after Isabella?"

I shrugged. "Not my job to speculate. It's my job to find out how and fix it."

Ryan seemed to sigh for a moment. And I knew I'd gotten that response wrong. This was the part where I was supposed to engage in conversation, to speculate and see if we could come up with some wild theories. We were supposed to bro it up here. I wasn't really good at that. Dylan walked in the conference room next, followed by Rafe and then Noah. Noah's face said it all: a mask of no nonsense and what the fuck.

When everyone was seated, he turned to me first. "Where are we now?"

I responded with a direct stare. "I've got all routes blocked. Attacks are stopped for now, but they'll come back. I'll need some more processing power to really lock it down. And honestly, like I've said before, I think it's time we go to a completely offline network. It's much harder to hack and if they want to hack us, they'll have to come directly here. It's a lot more expensive, but it's safer. Right now, they hit us hard."

I left out the part about how they'd been coming for us for weeks. That I'd managed to stave off all other comers. I also managed to leave out that I knew exactly who the attack was coming from. There was nothing Noah or anyone could do about it anyway. When the Family wanted you, they usually got you.

Well, not this time. I was going to protect this family. No matter what it took.

Noah pondered this for a moment. "Okay let's do it… whatever the expense. We can afford it, but it worries me having a self-contained unit. More secure, but if we're off-site harder for us to affect the outcome out in the field."

I nodded. "This is true. We'll need mobile command units every time we go out. It'll be a little riskier for those who are in the field, but overall, you'll be more protected."

Noah nodded. "Fair enough."

As the meeting went on, I could feel the tension vibrating around the table. They were all looking at me, wondering why I hadn't been able to protect us from the kind of attacks we'd seen. They were wondering if I'd lost my touch.

They should be worried. Maybe I had lost my touch.

No. You didn't lose your touch. They're just coming for you with everything they've got.

After going over our open cases and trying to determine if it was best to temporarily move the women and Isabella out of the penthouse to somewhere safer, the meeting adjourned. I stayed for a moment longer, finishing up some of the work I had. But when I was done, I bypassed the living room and was walking past the kitchen when I heard Rafe and Noah talking.

"You can't say you're not concerned."

"He's got it together. He'll be fine."

It was Rafe's voice that said, "Are you sure about that? You guys get all on my case about, you know, the not-killing-people-thing. He's barely restrained, Noah. He's hanging on by a thread. I think we're past the point of thinking that everything will just turn out okay. You should have seen him. It's not that he's a trained killer. We all are. It's not that I don't think he'll protect every one of us with his life. Well, except me, because he's already proven that he will. It's in his eyes, Noah. His monster is ready to come out to play. And when it does, I'm not sure we'll be able to stop him."

Noah's voice was harsh when he answered. "I seem to remember not so long ago when that was you. Your monster came out to play lots of times. As a matter of fact, you, brother, nearly killed me."

Rafe's voice went low. "That was different. *I* was under control. *I* was protecting my sister. Matthias is different. Look, I don't know what deal you made to get him out of ORUS, and trust me, I understand where the kid is coming from. I understand that pain. I understand the killer inside him. But we can't pretend anymore, Noah. Pretending is dangerous. He needs to see someone."

My heart hammered against my ribs. I was certain that at any moment, I would feel the internal splintering of my bones. I wasn't sure what was worse; knowing that Rafe could see that I didn't have control anymore (if I ever had), or knowing that Noah was defending me without knowing the truth.

I *was* losing control. Everything I'd been doing—the lies of omission I'd been telling, my need to go after Father and the Family—it was putting everything at risk. And the only person who could see it was the person most like me.

In the kitchen, I heard Noah's low, "Fuck off, Rafe. He saved my daughter's life. He stopped some psychopath from taking her."

"I know. I was there. I watched him do it. He did everything he could to protect Isabella, and I'm grateful for that. All I'm saying is that we're getting to that point. The kid needs more help than we can provide. Otherwise, it might not be safe to have him here."

"End of conversation, Rafe."

"You really think it's safe having him just down the hall from your daughter? My niece?"

"The kid is loyal. He would never hurt Isabella."

"What I'm saying is he might not know it if he did."

Despite the pain dancing through my gut as I made it the rest of the way down the hall to my room, I knew one thing; Rafe was right about me. I was dangerous to have around.

It was only a matter of time before I lost control of the monster inside me.

———

Gemma

WAS THIS OUTFIT DEMURE ENOUGH?

I certainly hoped so. I glanced down at myself. The skirt was made of polyester and rayon. Not an A-line, but not form fitting. It was just a skirt, plain in color — navy blue, slightly boxy. I'd worn a white shirt primly tucked in, one of the buttons missing in the middle deliberately, with the sleeves of the blouse rolled up.

Demure would work. It was what I needed. I needed

to be plain, nondescript. If I was facing that killer again, I could show nothing of who I really was. It would be an amazing feat if I could walk into this den of killers and pull this off.

My jaw still smarted, and I gently worked it as the elevator lifted me floor by floor. My head was still ringing from the fight yesterday. He'd gotten in several hits. I'd gotten by without any sewing, but I'd needed glue stiches on my cheekbone. He hadn't broken any bones, but bugger, everything hurt.

My nose hadn't been broken, but damn he packed a punch. But despite all the pain, it was as if he'd done everything he could not to kill me. Even as he'd strangled me. There'd been control...barely leashed control, but still.

The question was, why?

I'd seen it in his eyes. Every hit, every kick, every movement had been carefully calculated, as if he wanted to draw out the kill. *Or*, as if he wanted to keep me alive. But that was ridiculous. Why would someone associated with the Family want to keep me alive? The Family was filth— the worst of the worst. But it was clear that Perseus had held back once he realized I was female.

In my experience, anyone associated with them was pure evil. And I didn't know how Blake Security fit in to all of this, but if they had someone the Family wanted, I had to operate as if they were pure evil as well.

I'd done my research on them. Their backgrounds were as expected; law enforcement, military, etc. Bland; nothing stood out as red flags. Of course it wouldn't. That was their cover.

Stop overthinking it. Get the job done.

From my purse, I pulled out a handkerchief and ran my thumb over it. God, this was going to hurt something awful. I hoped I got the dosage right because I needed enough time to put the handkerchief back into my purse before they found me. And I couldn't just stage myself because if I was right, there were cameras up above in the elevator, watching me, tracking my every move. I made it a point to fidget, to adjust my clothing... to shake my shoulders as if I were crying. If only there were Academy Awards given out for fake clients, I would certainly deserve one.

The thing was I didn't have to fake, my fear. I knew I was going to see that guy again. I knew I was going to have to look into the blackness of his eyes. I knew that if he ever found out, if any of them found out, I was as good as dead.

But Andromeda had trained me. I knew how to do this. Get in. Get close to the target. Get out.

The mission statement on their website said, "*Blake*

Security thrives to provide the ultimate security service for all clients, no matter your circumstances. We believe in protection for everyone. If you have a problem, call us." Well, I did have a problem. Too bad they didn't know my problem was one of their own.

The elevator flew past the 15th floor and I braced myself. The penthouse was next. I made a production of scratching at my nose with my opposite hand, careful not to put the chloroform up into my nose too early. I scratched at it and wiggled my nose and tossed my head back so that the camera would catch me. It was all about the show.

I wiggled my nose again and scratched at it and then made a production of sneezing into the handkerchief before I inhaled deeply. Quickly, I tucked the chloroformed handkerchief back into my purse and forced myself to take a long breath. Just as the door to the elevator opened, I stepped out.

In front of me was hardwood floor. To my right was what looked like a reception office or something. To my left was the door I'd come in through when I broke in the previous evening. In front of me was a glass entrance to the foyer. Because it was business hours, the door opened easily.

Just as my head began to spin, I looked around and

saw someone big with dark hair coming toward me. He frowned. "Can I help you?"

I tried to nod. My head spun. *Oh God.* My stomach lurched and I knew it was going to be bad. The chloroform was starting to do its work. How was it I always forgot the effects of chloroform on me? I was going to be sick.

The blackness edged in on my peripheral vision, and despite needing to feel weak and incapacitated, I still fought it. The part of me that was a fighter—the part of me that understood that while unconscious, I couldn't fight for my life; the part of me that knew I was going to come face-to-face with the man I was supposed to kill— fought the drug. But fighting it was no good because I was going to go out. And just like that, as the dark-haired man frowned and reached for me, I collapsed and darkness took over.

6
———

Matthias

I HAD JUST GOTTEN SETTLED behind my desk and opened my laptop when my phone chimed. It was tempting to ignore it but with everything going on, I couldn't afford to. With my luck, something else was on fucking fire.

Noah—*Need to see you. I'm in my office.*

I groaned. There were only a million things I needed to do right now after such a massive security breach, but Noah was the one person I couldn't ignore. And I definitely didn't want to give the other man a reason to come looking for me. Most of the crew avoided my rooms, giving me the isolation I needed to function. But if I didn't show up, Noah would have no problem hunting me down. My mentor was a smart guy and had razor-sharp intuition. He'd probably figured out that I had overheard his conversation with Rafe earlier.

Whatever.

I shoved back from the desk in annoyance. They weren't a bunch of hens that needed to stand around talking about their bloody feelings all day. Rafe thought I was a psychopath. So what? I swallowed the lump in the back of my throat. It shouldn't matter to me if the guy thought I was a psycho. Hell I'd been called much worse.

I'd even thought much worse myself.

But it did matter. I rubbed a hand over my face in frustration. It was unusual for me to give a shit what anyone thought of me. Making friends and being liked hadn't exactly been high on my priority list. *Ever.* But Rafe was someone Noah respected, even when he wanted to kill the bloke. No matter how you swung it, the dude was a badass. Not only that but Rafe had managed something that only a handful of others had done: he'd built a successful life outside of ORUS.

Yes, Noah had done it, but that was different. I snorted. My friend would balk at the descriptor but Noah wasn't like the rest of them. Assassin or not, he was good; a true protector and the hero type. I just wasn't cut from that cloth. I'd always had a streak of darkness even before ORUS cut out what was left of my soul.

My phone rang then, and I grunted. "I'm coming," I muttered but didn't bother answering. I just walked out into the hall.

The first thing I saw was Rafe cradling a woman gently in his arms. Her dark hair was covering her face but what I could see of her skin was covered in bruises. My steps quickened until I paused and knelt next to them on the floor.

"Is she all right? Is Breckner on his way?"

Rafe glanced over at me briefly before looking back down at the woman. "Can you call him?"

I pulled my phone out and sent a message to the doctor we kept on call for various emergencies. Considering all the shit that had gone down over the past two years alone, I figured Dr. Breckner had more than earned the outrageous salary Noah paid him for his services.

I put my fingers to her pulse, pleased to find it beating sure and strong beneath my fingers.

"She came off the elevator and just collapsed. It's obvious why she's here." Rafe's face darkened as he motioned to the bruising on her arms and neck.

Just then the woman stirred, tossing her head from

side to side as if she was in pain. Her eyes opened and locked on me.

I'd seen enough movies to have seen the traditional bullshit romance scenes where an atypically attractive guy and girl locked eyes and moved in slow motion as they discovered they'd found their soulmate.

I'd always thought it was the corniest bullshit ever but in the space of a heartbeat, I discovered that maybe this was one thing the movies didn't get completely wrong.

My breath stuttered in my chest as her eyes roamed over me. It was strange, but I found myself unable to move as she made her mental evaluation of me. It was suddenly vitally important that I not do anything to scare her. I wasn't sure where this sudden protective streak came from, but it caught me completely off guard.

Then she blinked and the breath I'd been holding left my lungs in a great rush of air. She coughed slightly and let out a little wheeze.

Rafe moved to sit her up, and his movement alerted her to where she was. She glanced at him in alarm and then struggled against his hold. Her soft whimpers struck me right in the heart.

"Leave her alone. You're hurting her," I growled.

Rafe narrowed his gaze at me. "Take it easy, kid. I'm

not trying to hurt her. We need to move her so the doctor can look at her."

I looked around, stunned to see the doctor had arrived and I hadn't even noticed. Noah stood with Dr. Breckner watching us with interest. Heat rushed to my face, but it didn't stop me from taking her into my arms and carrying her over to the couch in the living area. By the time I placed her down gently, she'd passed out again. My heart accelerated wildly at the thought that she might be hurt even worse than we'd thought.

"She passed out again. What does that mean? Could she have a head injury?" I demanded as the doctor appeared at her side.

Breckner placed his black bag on the floor next to the couch before peering at her. Just seeing him kneeling next to the girl, who seemed even more help-less lying on the couch, made me twitchy.

"Just be careful with her, understand?"

The doctor blinked several times in surprise but nodded slowly before I stepped back. I looked over in time to catch Noah and Rafe exchanging glances but didn't have time to care that they were probably wondering what the hell was up with me.

All my focus and attention was on one raven-haired girl whose name I didn't even know.

It was torture to watch her go through the exam.

She cried out and woke briefly when Breckner palpated her ribs. I almost had my hand around the doctor's throat before Noah caught me around the chest.

"Whoa, dial it back. Let him do his job."

I closed my eyes, hating the feel of my friend's arm around me but needing it at the same time. Noah was good, but he was also strong. Strong enough to keep me from doing anything crazy.

It was frightening to realize that I wasn't in charge of my own control center right then. Something about this woman fired all my protective instincts. She reminded me of someone. *She's not Gigi.*

I'd hate to put the good doctor in a coma when all he was doing was checking her out.

"Vitals are strong. Nothing appears to be broken," Breckner said shakily, keeping one eye on me even as he spoke to Noah. "Bruises on her collarbone, ribs, thighs. They look to be about a day old, roughly." He turned back to the woman. "Ah, you're awake."

We all paused and looked down at the woman lying on the couch. Both eyes were now open and fixed determinedly on me.

"All right, love?"

Her eyes widened at the sound of my voice before darting around the room. She probably had no idea where she was since we'd moved her to a different room than the one she'd entered.

"It's all right. You're safe now."

And I'd do whatever was necessary to make sure she stayed that way.

———

Gemma

I FOUGHT TO BREATHE. Every inhale took concentration. Then I could focus on my body, which currently felt loose. Disconnected. Voices nearby filtered through.

Even though I couldn't open my eyes yet, I could hear them. Distinctly male voices that I didn't recognize.

They were talking about me. *Bruises on her collarbone. Ribs. Thighs.*

As if the words touched me physically, I became suddenly aware of the soreness in each of the affected areas. Aching pain radiated from every inch of my skin and my heart rate increased as my fear increased. I had to wake up. *Now.*

It was like swimming to the surface of a lake. I struggled against the lethargy currently making me feel like I had an elephant sitting on my chest.

My eyes opened and I blinked frantically. Where was

I? I was resting on something soft, and the man I'd heard talking was alarmingly close. He said something to me, but I didn't hear. All of my attention was on the man across the room.

The target.

My brain was still a little foggy, but I suddenly had a vision of him carrying me. Had he been the one to catch me when I passed out? No, that didn't make sense. I distinctly remembered the man who'd been waiting in the hallway when I'd gotten off the elevator. He'd been older. Insanely hot, but definitely older.

This guy, *the target*, I corrected myself, didn't look much older than I was. Which was interesting. He didn't look like he'd been alive long enough to be on the Family's shit list.

Then he spoke and things started to make sense.

"All right, love?"

His accent was just like the one I took such great pains to conceal: British. East End. Maybe south London. That made a lot more sense then. He must have had dealings with the Family and then come over here to the States to hide out. Maybe the hot older guy was a cousin who was hiding him or something. I made a mental note to find out the dynamic going on behind the scenes. It would only make things easier if I understood what I was up against.

"It's all right. You're safe now." His dark eyes held mine and I felt the conviction of his statement through and through. No matter what else happened, I'd be okay as long as he was there.

My head swam, and I thought back to earlier. I must have used too much chloroform. It was only supposed to make me passing out seem more convincing. I wasn't supposed to be unconscious for very long. But the heaviness in my head was getting worse instead of better. Panicked, I sought out the man who made me feel safe. The one who would protect me.

His dark eyes were worried as they locked on mine. While his lips were moving, I couldn't hear anything. But he looked worried. Strangely enough I didn't like that. Part of me wanted to put my hand to his brow, smooth the worry line there.

The next time I woke, I was in a bed.

"You're awake. Good. I was starting to get worried." The target was sitting next to me on the bed. This close, I could truly see how young he was. But he had strong features and his eyes... I swallowed nervously. He had the kind of eyes that could see right through you. I would have to be careful what I said around him. This wasn't the kind of man you could lie to without penalty.

"Where am I?" I asked, feigning confusion.

"Blake Security. Do you remember coming to see us

earlier?" He leaned over and picked up a glass of water from the nightstand and offered it to me.

I took a careful sip from the glass. My throat felt like sandpaper. "How long was I asleep?"

"A little more than an hour. Your body needs time to recover." His gaze darkened as he looked down at my bare arms.

If only he knew the truth. The bruises that horrified him were ones caused by his hands. I almost felt guilty working his sympathy this way. I definitely wasn't a wilting rose by any means. But I had a mission and if this was my only way in, I would take it.

"There are a lot of things my body needs," I murmured.

His face flushed immediately, and I giggled nervously at the double entendre. He really was unbelievably good looking with his strong features but boyish expressions. The scowl on his handsome face seemed out of place. Almost like he was trying to temper his good looks and youth.

Hell, maybe he was. If he was involved with the Family in any way, he clearly wasn't a choirboy. They were a ruthless organization but they were smart. Most of the people on their shit list were just as dirty as they were. After all, messing with ordinary citizens just increased the chances of being on law enforcement's radar. Which was something the Family preached they must avoid at all costs.

"Um, I just meant that I need a safe place to sleep for the night. That's why I'm here. I heard Blake Security helps people like me. People who need to hide."

He nodded. "We do. One of our core missions is to shelter those who need it. If someone is threatening you, we can protect you and help you establish a new life under a new identity. If that's what you want."

I smiled. Over the course of my ORUS training I'd had multiple names and identities. Not that he knew any of that.

"I would appreciate that. My father has no idea where I am, and that's how it needs to stay."

His jaw clenched. "Your father did this to you?"

I didn't answer. Better to let him assume as much as possible. Harder to get caught in a lie that way.

"You don't have to talk about it yet. Rest. I'll bring you something to eat. There's time enough for all of that later."

I leaned back against the pillows with a sigh. "Thank you for all of this. Really."

He paused next to the bed and watched me with the strangest expression. If I'd known him better, I almost would think it was fondness.

"It's what we do. Miss—I don't even know your name."

"Gemma," I whispered, using my ORUS-issued government identity.

He nodded, not remarking on the fact that I hadn't provided a last name. "Well, Gemma, you don't need to thank me. Us. The whole team. We're happy to help." He flushed slightly and then turned to go.

"Wait!" I sat up suddenly, my hand out as if to catch him. "You didn't tell me your name."

He paused briefly at the door and looked over his shoulder. "Matthias, Matthias Weller."

I sagged back against the pillows but there was a smile on my face. Matthias. A nice name for who I knew was a very dangerous man.

7

___

Matthias

I watched her sleep, wondering even as I did it why I couldn't seem to take my eyes from her face. She was beautiful, that much was apparent even with the motley assortment of bruises covering her cheek and nose.

Her dark hair was thick and looked like it would be soft if I buried my face in it. Not that I'd ever done anything like that. I shifted, uncomfortable with the direction of my thoughts. Sexual thoughts were normal for guys my age, sure, but with the kind of sick shit I'd grown up seeing, I'd tried to deaden that part of my humanity as much as possible.

What was it about this girl?

"How is she?" Oskar's voice floated over from the doorway.

I turned slightly so I could keep an eye on her while responding. "Better. Whatever Breckner gave her seems to have helped with the pain. She's sleeping easier now."

"Good. That's... good. You know I can stay with her if you want to get something to eat. Or whatever."

He entered the room then, approaching the bed hesitantly. I had to quell the urge to tell him to get the fuck out.

Do you hear yourself? Calm the fuck down before she wakes up. Also, remember that thing about you being a psychopath? Stop it.

If the tight feeling around my lips was any indication, I was baring my teeth like an animal. The idea of scaring her doused the panic inside a bit and I took a deep breath. Then Oskar moved a little closer and I jumped to my feet.

"Back off, mate."

I didn't like anyone else getting too close to her, especially while she was unconscious and vulnerable. It was a ridiculously over-the-top reaction. I knew it. But I couldn't help myself. Someone had done this to her, and for some reason I felt like I was the one who had to protect her. I didn't want anyone else alone in the room with her. She felt like my responsibility. Something inside drove me to stay near her, watch over her. Almost like she was... mine.

As if the other man could hear my thoughts, Oskar crossed his arms. "Rafe said you were acting weird around her. What's up with that?"

I growled. "Nothing. I just want to make sure she's okay. Rafe needs to worry about his own woman."

Oskar chuckled. "I'm pretty sure he's taking good care of Diana. But if you want to tell him that, I won't stop you. That fight would be better than pay-per-view."

I grimaced at the thought. The last time I'd gone toe-to-toe with Rafe I'd ended up confined to a hospital bed for a week. Oskar had escaped with only a dislocated shoulder, but Jonas had almost gone blind. It would be different now because I knew his weaknesses. I was also willing to kill him. He was not willing to kill me.

"Whatever," I muttered before shifting to put my body between Oskar and the woman asleep on the bed.

The woman who made me feel like I could take on a whole team of Rafes to protect her. The woman I was pretty sure had just given me a fake name.

"Do we know who she is? Did she give Rafe a name?"

Oskar shook his head. "No. We have no idea who she is. We searched her bag and coat and there was no identification. Her phone is one of those cheap burner phones. She's definitely running from something. Or somebody."

I tensed and stepped back hoping a little distance would keep me from reaching for her. What the hell was going on with me? It felt like my skin was electrified at just the thought of someone hurting her. For someone who made it a rule not to get too close to anyone, it was an uncomfortable feeling, like my body had grown one size too big for my skin.

Oskar eyed me. "What the hell is wrong with you? Dude, you're freaking out a bit."

I ran my hands through my hair in frustration. "I don't know why I'm reacting this way."

Oskar smirked. "I can explain it to you. See when little boys like little girls, their pee pee gets hard."

I punched him in the chest and then swung for the face but Oskar managed to block that one.

"Shit! I forget how fast you are. Little fucker." Oskar winced as he rubbed his sternum. "That actually hurt. You pack a punch for such a little guy."

I snorted. I was several inches over six feet. Only Oskar would refer to me as a 'little guy.'

"Anyway, I'm not here just to bust your balls," Oskar said. "Noah needs to see you."

I glanced behind him again. All the commotion we'd

made hadn't woken the girl on the bed, thankfully. I turned back to Oskar and eyed the big German skeptically.

"Isn't there anyone else who can sit with her? Where's Lucia?" Noah's wife was sweet and would be a nice, calming presence in case the girl woke before I came back.

It briefly occurred to me that I should feel weird asking for Lucia to come here. After all, it wasn't that long ago that I'd been nursing an unrequited crush on the petite brunette. But I'd known all along that she wasn't for me. Even before I'd acknowledged it, I'd known she was meant for Noah. That fact had been obvious to everyone except her.

"She's in the living room. I'll ask her to come. JJ is here, too." Oskar smirked.

I hesitated. Lucia's best friend, Jessica Jones, was super loud and brazen as hell. I had no issues with Lucia watching over the sleeping girl, but if she woke up to JJ's brand of crazy, she'd probably run away and never come back.

"I'm not sure if that's better or worse."

Oskar raised an eyebrow. "Well, I can stay if you'd rather—"

I brushed past him. "Never mind. It probably doesn't matter anyway."

Then I paused when I heard Oskar say, "Looks like someone is awake."

I turned and paused when the woman on the bed opened her eyes and looked right at me.

It definitely matters, I thought.

———

Gemma

I'D FALLEN ASLEEP AGAIN.

I took in a deep breath, trying to clear my head. Clearly my plan hadn't been too well thought out since I'd been inside the belly of the beast for hours now and spent the majority of that time asleep.

Not exactly the ideal way to get the jump on the target, eh?

I quelled the first stirrings of panic at the thought of how much time had been wasted. That wouldn't help me now. I just had to move forward with the plan.

Peeling one eye open, I watched the dark haired man, happy that he was facing away from me. His words were aggressive, but yet I still got the sense that the blond man he was arguing with was a friend.

That didn't stop him from throwing a punch though.

I tensed on the bed, hoping they wouldn't notice that

I'd woken up again. They were talking and that's exactly what I wanted them to do. Maybe they'd give up some information that would be helpful if they didn't know I was awake. Trying not to move too much, I strained to listen to their conversation.

Then I heard, *'Looks like someone is awake,'* and I knew the ruse was up. I opened my eyes to two pairs of equally intense eyes, one dark and one ice blue.

Holy hotness, Batman. I was surrounded by testosterone. What was up with this place? The guy I'd first met when I got off the elevator had been insanely hot, too. What kind of security company was this? Or maybe it was a front for a male escort agency. I snorted softly at the thought.

"Hi," I muttered finally, still a little annoyed that the blond guy had seen through my pretense.

The dark haired one slowly sat on the edge of the bed I was lying on. His eyes didn't leave my face as he moved, and I found myself unable to look away. Dimly, I heard the door close and knew the blond man had left us alone, but I still couldn't break eye contact.

With Matthias.

His name swam through my mind and I thought back to everything I'd learned before the Family sent me on this mission. The name wasn't familiar and I wondered again exactly what he could have done to have earned the wrath of an international criminal organization.

"I fell asleep again," I finally said, pulling my eyes away from his.

"You needed the rest. I didn't mind watching over you." Matthias didn't smile as he said it, but a warm flush raced through me at the words. I imagined him sitting next to me, watching me sleep in that intense way of his, protecting me. On someone else it probably would have come across a bit stalkerish, but somehow on him, it fit. He seemed intense and protective. *And deadly... don't forget deadly.*

What must it be like to be the sole focus of his attention? To have a man so into you, that he was fascinated even with watching you sleep. Especially a man like this. I peeked over at him again. It was impossible to pretend I was unaffected by that face. He was so handsome.

I could feel the slight blush on my cheeks and pushed my hair back from my face, hoping to disguise my reaction to him.

This wouldn't do. If I was going to have any chance of taking this guy on, it would have to be away from his home turf. Here, he was in his element and had plenty of backup. I needed to take him off guard.

"I should be going." I sat up all the way, pushing the light blanket off my legs. I imagined him covering me with it, tucking the edges around my body to keep me warm.

Oh yeah, I needed to go. The man had me completely off my game, daydreaming about him tucking me into bed!

"Wait. I don't think that's a good idea. You came to us for help, so let us help you." Matthias looked at the bruising on my arms and raised his hand but paused before touching me.

Could he feel it, too? This heat between us? I watched his hand greedily, wanting him to touch me but fearing I'd just melt into a puddle of goo if he did.

"I can't. I shouldn't have come here."

Matthias moved back as I swung my legs over the side of the bed. I sneaked a look up at him, inordinately pleased to see his eyes hurriedly flick away from my legs. So he was feeling it, too. It was a good thing, because I could use his attraction to further my mission.

But he could use your attraction against you, too. My rational mind was screaming for me to proceed slowly and with caution. Despite how innocuous he seemed, this man, Matthias, was an enemy of a powerful organization which meant he obviously wasn't what he seemed. If I wasn't careful, he'd get the upper hand and I'd be no better off than when I'd started.

"I can't let you leave." Matthias knelt next to me and took my hands.

I startled at the contact, and my eyes flew to his. I sucked in a breath at what I saw there. Desire, yes, but something bigger. Something I couldn't define.

"I really should go home."

"And I'll take you. Later," he added quickly. "Just let our physician check you out again to make sure that you're really okay. Once I'm sure of that, I'll take you home myself. Deal?"

It sounded reasonable but the look in his eyes clearly spelled out that he was up to something. I figured he'd grill me about who had hurt me. But to my surprise, he stood and extended his hand without saying a word.

It was shock that made me take it.

Yeah, tell yourself that.

I shook my head as I stood, struck at once with just how big he was; built lean like a runner but tall, easily six inches taller than I was. My head would fit right on his shoulder if we were cuddled up.

Stop it. Think. You need a plan.

"Where are we going?" I asked.

"To the kitchen. You need to eat before the doctor looks at you again."

I pulled my hand from his, annoyed at how easily

he'd outmaneuvered me. I was supposed to be getting him out of here and onto neutral ground, but somehow he'd pushed me into eating dinner and getting seen by their doctor again. It was unnerving how he seemed to exert his will without much effort. I bet he was used to doing that with women. With a face and a body like his, he probably had girls falling in line to do whatever he wanted.

Not that I was jealous.

"I don't know about this."

He stopped and put a finger under my chin so I was forced to meet his eyes.

"You're safe with me, Gemma."

The sound of my government identity pulled me back into the present. ORUS was counting on me not to screw this mission up. The Family wouldn't be pleased if I didn't have something to report soon and Sabine's life depended on it. I had to get it together.

"I feel safe with you," I said.

His eyes flashed at my words, and I gulped. He looked entirely too pleased right now. And there was a traitorous part of me that really liked the idea of pleasing him.

"What if the doctor says I'm not okay?" I pushed, wanting to clarify exactly what I was agreeing to.

Matthias squeezed my hand gently. "Then I'm sure

we can find room for you to stay here overnight. Where you'll be safe."

Not ideal. I needed him away from here. But, thinking quickly, I smiled. It might be easier to catch him off guard if I was staying here. And all the other people around had to leave sometime, right?

"Okay," I whispered. "It would be nice to feel safe for once."

He looked pleased at my capitulation and I almost felt bad for deceiving him. But then I remembered that he wasn't what he appeared either.

So it looked like we had something in common after all.

8

———

Matthias

I ROLLED OVER AGAIN and punched my pillow. Sleep had never been an easy thing for me, but tonight it was proving particularly elusive. Calming my mind enough to allow myself to be vulnerable just wasn't going to happen when I had someone I needed to protect one door away.

I imagined Gemma in the room I'd given her, curled up in the queen-size bed. Was she warm enough? She'd only eaten a little. What if she woke up hungry in the middle of the night?

What if she woke up scared?

I grunted. Like I was the right one to reassure her or calm her fears. I ran a hand over my face. If that girl knew half the shit I'd done, I doubted she'd feel safe enough to close her eyes around me. If something or someone was a threat, I removed the threat. Simple. It wasn't just the way I'd been trained, it was, in my mind, the only logical step to be taken.

No wonder ORUS considered you one of their best assets. A born and bred killing machine.

Most of the time, I didn't dwell on the things I'd done. My mind wasn't wired that way. But there were times when I was forced to face my past, and then the world felt like it was going to collapse in on me. So better if I didn't examine the person I used to be... or just how easy it was to be that person.

Not for the first time, I wished I could be different, be the kind of man who'd know how to take care of a girl like that. The kind who knew the soft words and gentle phrases that would calm her and make her feel safe.

Unable to pretend that I was going to get any sleep any longer, I stood and stretched before padding barefoot over to my desk. With a few swipes and clicks, I woke my laptop and had the security feeds visible on the multitude of screens on the wall in front of me. My eyes danced over each image, scrutinizing the dark and silent rooms, hallways and stairwells that comprised Blake Security.

Ever since the breach, I'd shored up all the security and changed everyone's passwords but I was still on high alert. As my eyes kept coming back to the dark hallways, I realized one of the guys was awake and walking down the hallway near his room.

Near Gemma.

I tensed and moved closer to the screen. Could I really trust the other guys in the house? It was a hard lesson I'd learned in my youth. No one was truly your friend. They were only pretending until it was no longer advantageous for them. The only one I'd ever trusted was the only one I'd been unable to protect.

I blocked out the thoughts of Gigi. My failure to protect my only friend wasn't something I liked to think about.

The dark shape on the screen kept walking and passed Gemma's door before appearing on the screen in the kitchen. Once the lights were on, I could see Rafe digging in the refrigerator. Probably looking for a late night snack for Diana. She was expecting and had some seriously weird food cravings.

I smiled at the thought.

Things were different now. Noah, Jonas, Oskar and the other guys weren't like the people I'd grown up with in the Family. They weren't just paying lip service to their loyalty; these men had fought and bled beside me. None of them would take a woman I considered mine.

But she's not yours, is she?

The sly voice tormented me with the truth. Gemma wasn't my girlfriend; she wasn't my anything. Just a scared girl who needed protection. And that's what I'd give her.

A soft sound had me on my feet. I gaped as Gemma entered the room and then closed the door behind her. I'd been so lost in my thoughts that I hadn't noticed her leaving her room on the security feed.

"Hi," she finally said.

For a very long moment, we stared at each other. Her expression was hard to make out in the dim room but there was a lot I could get just from body language. She shifted from foot to foot and her fingers twisted in her long hair, the dark strands shiny and thick as they cascaded over her shoulder.

"What are you doing in here?" My voice sounded rusty even to my own ears and not all that friendly.

Jesus, I was already fucking this up. I cleared my throat and sat in my desk chair. After what she'd been through, she didn't need someone looming over her. I didn't even question it, my instinctive desire to make her feel safe and protected.

It was pretty much a given at this point that I'd give her whatever she needed. It should have terrified me, how one girl could command me so completely, and maybe under different circumstances it would. But in the thick of the emotion, I just knew it was what I was supposed to do.

"I can't sleep. It's so quiet here." She looked around my room and then back at her feet, like she was embarrassed to have been caught looking.

I wanted to tell her that she could look at whatever she wanted, that I'd slice open my chest and give her a view of my beating heart if it would take that haunted look from her face. But that might scare her even more than me standing over her, I thought with a grimace.

Was this what Noah, Jonas and Rafe had gone through? I smiled slightly. I'd been confused but simultaneously envious watching the men I'd looked up to, and come to think of as brothers, fall in love. It wasn't something I'd thought I was even capable of.

"It's the height," I commented, wanting her to look up at me again. I was desperate for her eyes on me. "We're so high above the ground that all the city sounds just fall away. It takes a while to get used to it."

She looked up then. "You'd think I'd appreciate it. After living with my father coming in drunk at all hours and raging, I should love the quiet."

My stomach tightened at her casual mention of living with a raging maniac. It took quite a bit of willpower to push down the urge to go hunt the bastard down right then and bring his head back on a pike to present to her.

"No matter how shitty our environment, if it's what you're used to, then something different will always feel foreign."

She nodded. "Yeah. I woke up feeling like I just needed to see something familiar. Something safe."

And she'd come to me...

I had to bite my lip to hold down the rush of pleasure that screamed through my system at her words. The intense pride warred with a shot of desire so strong it went straight to my cock. I sucked in a short breath, taken off guard by how quickly I got hard for her. Sure my face was flaming, I tugged at the T-shirt I was wearing, grateful it was long enough to conceal the barge pole sticking out of my lap.

"You don't mind, do you?" she asked.

And even though I knew it was going to take Herculean strength not to act on the hard on currently trying to lead me across the room, I kept my face impassive as I motioned for her to come closer.

"Feel free to hang in here. I usually don't sleep much. Or at all," I muttered.

She grinned at that. "Me either. But it'll be nice not to be alone." Then she walked across the room and sat on the edge of my bed, tucking her legs underneath her.

And I wished I'd worn a sweatshirt. Or a blanket. Because there was no way I could hide my delight at having her in my bed.

———

Gemma

IT WAS A CALCULATED RISK. I had gone over all of the scenarios. Leaving and trying again to break in. Waiting until morning and then inviting him out. Or giving him my number and seeing if he would pursue me.

But in the end, when hunting you had to either catch an animal off guard or stalk it down in its own lair. He wasn't going to be caught off guard easily.

But it turned out that his lair wasn't so difficult to infiltrate.

"Sorry. I probably should have asked if you minded," I said as I made myself completely at home on his bed.

The joke was on me though because I hadn't counted on the effect his scent would have on me. His bed smelled like him, subtle hints of amber and wood smoke, like testosterone distilled into its most potent form. I almost whimpered. If a perfumery could bottle this scent it would become the new female Viagra.

I wanted to roll around on the bed and cover myself in his smell. Then touch myself later while moaning his name.

There was no way he could know what I was thinking. But at the sight of me curled up in his bed, Matthias sat up straighter and his eyes ran over my body with such intensity that I could actually feel it. The hair on the back of my arms raised, and I gulped.

The man's eyes were dangerous. I felt like my panties might incinerate just from the heat of his gaze.

"You don't have to ask. You already know you can have whatever you want from me." His voice was deeper, rougher and that combined with the provocative words made me bold.

"Anything?"

He didn't answer, just kept staring at me until I blushed so hard I worried steam would come from my ears. Matthias seemed like the type who kept his feelings under wraps. I'd seen that when he was interacting with the others, especially the big blond man. He had responded almost robotically, as if showing any emotion was a weakness.

But with me it was different. *Yeah right*, I thought

sarcastically. *He's different with you because you're so special, huh?*

But it was true. Matthias telegraphed everything he was thinking and feeling when he talked to me. Right now his posture and the feral look on his face screamed S-E-X.

If we were two animals in the wild, I wouldn't be one bit surprised if he threw me to the ground and mounted me right here.

Unable to bear the intensity of his direct gaze, I lowered my eyes. This was the perfect opportunity for me to dig, to ask him questions. He was open to it and if I asked him about himself, he'd probably tell me. But surprisingly what came out of my mouth wasn't connected to my plan at all. Instead it was what I, the real person behind the mission, wanted.

"Would you just... hold me?" Immediately after asking, I bit my lip, uncomfortable feeling so vulnerable.

With everything that had gone down over the past few weeks, finding out Sabine was in danger, getting my mission, getting my counter mission from ORUS and then landing in the States, I realized that I really was craving a little comfort.

Matthias didn't answer but stood at once, his hands tugging at his shirt awkwardly.

Was he actually going to do it?

My mouth fell open slightly, but then I scooted over eagerly. It was so wrong that I was looking forward to this, but if he was willing to wrap those strong arms around me again, I wasn't going to question it. Especially since I'd been denied the pleasure of remembering him carrying me earlier. Whatever their doctor had given me for the pain had really knocked me out.

"Do you mind if I get comfortable?" Matthias asked.

I nodded, not sure what he meant and then gaped when he reached over his head and yanked his shirt off. He did it in the absentminded way that guys always did it, a quick motion with one hand, but it was somehow the sexiest thing I'd ever seen.

"You have tattoos?" I blurted when I got my first unobstructed view of his chest.

He didn't have full sleeves or anything that would show when he wore a regular shirt, but his entire torso was a map of ink. I sat up, intrigued by this intimate look at a guy who presented a front as straight-laced as a corset.

"What do they all mean? Did they hurt? How many do you have?"

He blinked at me, and I laughed softly.

"Sorry. That was a lot of questions." I watched with open fascination as he sat on the edge of the bed.

"It's okay. Usually I don't talk about them but... it's

okay." He glanced at me and then pointed to the hour-glass inked over his heart. "This one I got after I lost someone. She was... It was my fault. I got this to remind me that we never know how much time we have. Every second is a gift."

I exhaled, overwhelmed by the emotion in his voice. I had no idea who he was talking about, of course, but whoever she was, she was lucky. It was a bitter pill, but truthfully, if I bit it one of these days there weren't many who'd mourn me.

Hell, there weren't many who knew my real name.

"And that one?" I reached out tentatively and touched the roman numerals over his ribs.

He shuddered when my fingers touched his skin. I jerked my hand back but he reached out and grabbed my wrist.

"No. Touch me." It came out as a tortured whisper.

I marveled that what would be a pervy request from any other guy just seemed like an honor coming from him. It didn't take much to intuit that not many people got close enough to touch him. Some of the expressions I'd seen on his face so far directed at the other guys were so murderous I doubted many would try to cross him. But with me, he just watched me through slitted eyes, tracking my every movement like he was anticipating my touch.

I was too.

Matthias shifted slightly and the motion brought him up against my backside. Heat pulsed between us and I had to resist the urge to plaster myself against him. As it was, I couldn't resist rubbing against him a little. Then I froze.

He was huge. And hard.

And *huge*. Had I mentioned that part?

I swallowed hard. Holy shit. Just what had I gotten myself into? It wasn't like it was the first time I'd been this close to a guy. I wasn't a nun. But the hot make out sessions I'd had with previous guys I'd dated had always ended right around the time I could feel their arousal.

After the way I'd grown up and the things I'd seen since training with ORUS, men hadn't been high on my 'must trust' list. There were simply too many unknown factors and too many possibilities for harm if you let down your guard enough to get naked with someone.

Andromeda had always been clear that no one could be trusted and that I was to regard everyone with suspicion until after a full background check. Even then, it was best to proceed with caution.

Not exactly the best recipe for a relationship.

But more important than any of that, I really hadn't wanted any of those guys. They'd been cute enough and nice guys but nothing that made me willing to take a risk.

But here with Matthias, I experienced something completely new. A rare feeling of trust combined with explosive chemistry put me in new territory. *I wanted him.*

And I really wanted to see what he was hiding in those sweatpants.

So I rolled over and pressed closer to the big, hard tent in his pants.

9
____

Matthias

I swallowed hard. *Shit. Shit. Shit.*

I was hard. I could feel the throbbing length of myself twitching against my thigh. If I felt it, she had to feel it too. She was so damn close. And she smelled unbelievable. Like lavender and vanilla. I wanted to nestle closer and—*You are a twat. Stop thinking about her.*

My stupid dick... There was no containing that thing. Over the years, I'd learned Zen-like mastery over my cock. If I meditated, or if I worked out a lot, it kept me from thinking too much about sex. But, with her lying so close, feeling so soft, smelling so damn good, it was next to impossible. As a matter of fact, just think of the ocean. Nice calming breezes.

I tried. I honestly did. I thought of calming breezes, water—well, that just made me think of her. Wet and slick from the shower, or a pool, or the ocean... my hands sliding over her slick, naked flesh.

Bugger.

I squeezed my eyes shut. *Okay, water is not a good idea. Code... lines of intricate code. Think about the code, mate.*

That was more helpful. My brain tried to focus on how many lines of code it would take to hack the CIA. I forced my brain into the exercise to walk through the process and the difficulties getting to the firewall, the work of it, the challenge of it. Normally, something like this helped. Whenever I needed to get my monster back under control, this was what I did. I let my mind go to the thing that I knew best; computers. The ones and zeroes.

Except now, there was an anomaly... a *glitch.*

A line of code injected into my brain that I wasn't able to bypass, get rid of, demolish, move through, or walk around.

It was her. Her scent filled my nostrils, the scent wrapping around my neck like a cord, intoxicating me.

She rolled over more tightly into my body and I was

certain she could feel it.

And the fucking traitor, he twitched.

Her eyes went wide, and she shifted her gaze down before looking back up to my eyes. Gemma didn't move away though. She didn't look upset or angry. Instead... What was that?

She licked her bottom lip, and I swallowed hard to bite back the groan.

What the hell was wrong with me? She was hurt, and I was turned on by her? I knew I was a sick monster, but this... Jesus. There was something wrong with me— really, really wrong with me.

I wanted her more than I'd wanted anything in my life. The thing was I was content with just having her close to me and being able to breathe in the fresh, clean scent of her. Unlike me, she wasn't tainted. Her soul was pure, and she was beautiful on the inside. I could tell. There was something light about her.

Then what the hell is she doing here with you?

As much as I wanted her though, even if she wasn't hurt, it's not like I had any idea what the hell I was doing. I had zero experience in this area.

After the things I'd seen with the Family, the idea of sex turned me way the hell off. And those times that it didn't, well, I got tattooed or pierced something. Although, given that my cock was like steel in my sweatpants right now, I wasn't even sure that would calm the itch, the need scratching at the inside of my veins.

The first time I'd been kissed, it hadn't even been the real deal. Some lads in the Family had thought that it would be a grand idea to get me a slag. They'd always found it amusing that I hadn't had my cherry popped. So they'd thought it would be fun to hire me someone.

I didn't even remember her name, just that her perfume had been too sweet. When it wafted into my nostrils, it felt like a clawing parasite attaching itself to me. No caressing, no gentle seduction—all attack and attach.

I might not have remembered her name, but I still remembered that kiss. Too wet, too cold. And then she'd stuck her tongue in my mouth and she bit into my lip. I'd been young... *too* young. From what I remembered, she was in her twenties, but I knew from experience that she'd probably been forced to do all manner of things for whoever owned her. She'd been as helpless in that situation as I had been.

A shiver stole up my spine as I forcibly dislodged the memory. It didn't belong here in this bed with this woman.

My mother had worried about me. As soon as I hit ten or so, she'd rub my jaw and say I was too pretty for my own good. Even at that age, I'd known what she meant. That there was a high likelihood the Family would force me to become a rent boy.

That might have happened if I hadn't been so good with tech. I'd been more useful to them behind a monitor than sold to some john. So I'd managed to escape the worst parts of that life.

But given that I'd seen everything, knew what everyone was up to, and given the life my own mother had been forced into to work off her debt to the Family, I saw sex every day and the worst incarnations of it. Yeah, I was an adult now. I knew that most people felt love and attraction, and all those other things.

But I didn't know anything about it. I wasn't human. I wasn't one of the normals. I didn't get to have that.

I swallowed again, trying to dislodge the memory of that long-ago prostitute that had been paid to kiss me when I was thirteen. Yeah, I noticed girls, but I'd also noticed what would eventually happen with those girls, and I wanted no part of it.

But this girl, she was different. She made me want to wipe clean all the past shit.

I reached a hand up and caressed her bruised jaw. Gemma was different. *This* was different. *But you don't deserve this. Monsters don't get to have a fairy princess.* But she was so soft and so warm. It was as if her sweetness and innocence washed away the layers of grime and dirt that I felt were embedded beneath my skin. Like her cleanliness could somehow wash me clean.

"Matthias." Her voice was soft. Inquisitive.

"Gemma, this is really a bad idea."

"Why?"

"Because I haven't got a clue what I'm doing." The honesty had cost me. It hurt to be that vulnerable. But she rewarded me with the kind of smile I only dreamed about.

"Perfect. Neither do I. All I know is I just need you to kiss me."

And in that moment I knew that I couldn't stop myself.

I would give her whatever it was that she wanted. Because with her, the control I'd always been so proud of—the one thing that kept me from being one of the monsters, the one thing that kept me sane—snapped.

And there was no going back.

Gemma

THE DEVIL MADE me do it. If anyone ever asked what possessed me to brush my lips ever so softly against Matthias's, that would be my answer.

Everything about him was so stiff, so cold, except for when I woke to find him watching me, concern etched on his brow. And now, even though he held his body stiff, his muscles bunched. There was something about him that told me he was holding himself back.

When his shuddering breath blew out, I tucked in his hold. His eyes bore into mine, and his hands squeezed gently on my hip. "Gemma—"

"Yes?"

He swallowed hard. "This isn't a good idea."

"I know." And then I kissed him again. The same feather-light brush of my lips over his. He was right. It wasn't a good idea. As a matter of fact, it was a terrible idea. But right then, I couldn't help myself. I wanted more of that electric buzz skipping over my skin when I pressed my lips on his. I wanted his hand on my hip, firmer, tighter.

I wanted *him.*

You're insane. He nearly killed you. He's the target.

That was the rational part of my brain talking. The one that understood that one false move and I could die. The one that understood that not thirty-six hours ago, this guy was hell-bent breaking all the bones in my body.

I wouldn't look at those rational thoughts, because who needed rationality? At that moment, despite all my training and everything I'd been taught, all I wanted was him.

This could get you killed. But I didn't care. It was on the third brush of my lips that something in him broke. I could feel it. The tension between us coiled and then it sprung apart, and his lips crushed down over mine.

There was nothing gentle or soft about Matthias Weller. His lips were hard, bruising, his tongue seeking, probing, licking into my mouth and lighting me on fire from the inside out.

Everything about him set me on a collision course with ecstasy. Who cared if I died on the way there? I wanted more... more of this, more of his touch. I needed more.

With a growl, he rolled over me, his hips settling between my thighs and his hands fisting in my hair as if he was settling in to punish me for a good, long while with his lips.

I couldn't get enough. For every tightening of his hand in my hair, I arched my hips up. For every nip of his teeth on my bottom lip, I moaned into his mouth. For every infinitesimal rock of his hips into mine, I gasped.

When he gripped my hair tight and angled my head back, adjusting his kisses to slide along my jaw and my neck, I groaned low. "Matthias—"

His answer was a nip of his teeth against the column of my throat. There was something unskilled and unrestrained in the way he held me, in the way he kissed me, in the way his fingers played over my skin. He wasn't rough. Even though I could feel the urgency, the need, threading through him, he was still gentle with me, as if hyper-aware of my fragility. Little did he know that there was nothing fragile about me.

His lips over my skin were urgent, hot, and destructive. He nipped and sucked, and I knew I would be covered in stubble burn and hickeys if he kept that up, but I didn't care. I wanted his mark on me.

I knew I was losing it, forgetting what I'd come into Blake Security to do. Getting this close to any target was dangerous. I'd seen what had happened with Sabine. I knew what the Family wanted from this guy. But it was as if my body had shoved my brain off a cliff and had no intention of going after it because I wanted him.

He was big... really big. Considering how tall I was, when we were standing, the guy towered over me. And lying down in the king-size bed in the corner, he still had me practically braced up against the headboard. With a gentle slide of his hand over the nape of my neck, he dragged me down and shifted me so that my head wouldn't bang into the wood. Then he grabbed the pillow and adjusted it under my neck so I wouldn't have to strain.

He was turning me into a raging bonfire, and he still had the awareness to think about me being comfortable. If I couldn't feel the evidence of his hard length against my thigh, I would have to wonder just how interested he was.

I knew what he wanted, what he needed. And I needed it too. He had a hand in my hair, the other sliding down my body to the hem of the T-shirt I'd been given to wear. He yanked his lips from mine. His dark eyes bored into mine, asking me the silent question.

I couldn't have talked if I wanted to. My throat was constricted from need. So I gave him the only answer I could. I raised my hips and rotated them against the length of him.

I could only watch in fascination as the muscle in his jaw ticked and he sucked in a deep breath as if trying to get himself under control. Well, I didn't want him in control. I wanted him to be as desperate and needy and insistent as I was.

I didn't know what I was racing toward. I just knew that I needed it. And for some reason, Matthias Weller was the one who knew the way to my destruction, and I was happy to follow him like the pied piper.

With his gaze on mine, he eased his hand up the T-shirt. Were his hands shaking? When his thumb reached the edge of my simple cotton bra, he closed his eyes again and dropped his head to mine. I could hear him muttering something, but I couldn't understand what it was.

I was impatient, desperate, and he was torturing me? The hell he would. I arched my back in a desperate attempt to get him to move his hand. And what do you know? It worked. His large palm encased my whole breast, and I could hear it then: the long, drawn out, "Fuuuck."

He squeezed roughly, and I locked my legs around his waist. I didn't care if his movements were jerky or seemingly unpracticed. I just needed more. More touching from him. There had never been much time for anything like this.

Relationships, partnerships, sex—when was there time? I'd been so young when Andromeda took me in. I'd been raised to think about nothing but the missions. *Survival.* And even when I'd gone to normal school— high school—no one had ever made me curious enough. No one had ever made me want to risk every-thing for a touch before.

Why this guy? Why this beautiful face, his harsh eyes, and the vivid tattoos peppering his skin? Why did this guy trip my *oh-God-yes meter?*

Matthias's thumb traced over my nipple, and he pinched lightly.

I let out a low, keening yell, and he immediately swallowed the sound with a kiss, making me almost beg him to do it again just as hard as before.

With his fingers stroking my breast, his lips on mine, the length of him extended as he insistently rotated his hips into mine, I didn't know what to do. I didn't know how to move my body, but somehow this, the grinding of our hips against each other in this desperate need to touch and be touched, this felt right.

He moved his hand out of my hair and slid it down to my waist as if trying to keep me steady, but I couldn't stop. I needed more.

He tore his lips from mine and harsh pants ripped out of his throat. "Gemma—"

"God, please. I just—"

He kissed me again, and then adjusted his hips so the stiff length of his dick pressed just against my clit and I shuddered. *Oh, God, yes. Right fucking there.*

Between kisses he muttered "Fuck. Fuck me. Jesus." And I knew he could feel what I did; the desperate, echoing need. Even though we were separated by layers and layers of clothing, we might as well have been naked.

I could envision exactly what he would be doing to

me if we had our clothes off. He'd be sliding in and out of me, marking me as his, and staking his claim.

With a growl, he shifted his body down, kissing along my neck and collarbone gently, careful of my bruises, pausing only to lift my shirt up and over my breast.

While he was oh so careful with my skin, the same could not be said for the clothes I was wearing. He was none too gentle, and I heard the tearing of stitches of fabric. He paused to stare at the skin that was exposed and swallowed hard again. His gaze skimmed over my skin as if trying to get a picture of what he was seeing and encase it in his memory forever.

And then he dipped his head. His lips wrapped around a nipple and he sucked through the cotton.

"Oh God."

But he didn't stay long. I really wanted him to move the cloth aside so I could feel his lips on my bare skin.

Instead he kissed down my ribs to my stomach, pausing just at the edge of the scrub bottoms I'd been given. "Is—is this okay? Are you sure?"

He sounded so honest with his deep British accent, his words flowing over me like warm whiskey. "Yes. I'm sure."

He nodded. "Good. I've always wanted to do this."

10

———

Matthias

GEMMA TREMBLED IN MY ARMS, and I had to grit my teeth against the wave of lust threatening to take over any vestiges of control I had left.

Waves of ecstasy rolled through me, but I knew there was more. And I was so desperate for it. Desperate to feel her skin beneath mine. I needed whatever was coming next.

I flushed and I trembled as I warred with myself. There was a part of me that wanted to shred her clothes and rub myself all over her, relishing in the smooth softness of her skin.

Then there was the other part. The part of me who knew what I was, knew the things I'd seen, understood how tainted I was. She didn't deserve that.

But then I met her gaze and I could see the desire, tension, and desperation swirling, and I knew she was just as caught in the inferno as I was. I set my jaw as the decision was made for me.

Just this once, I could be a human being. I could let myself feel. *Please, God.* I wanted this so bad. I could give in. I could have her, just this once. Just one time feel what it was like to be normal, to feel something for someone.

My cock, the fucking twat, twitched against her thigh, and she groaned. I had to steel myself against the sound. A sound full of all the promises. The need churned through my veins like a raging river. I had to have her.

You don't deserve her.

Gemma ground her hips against me. *Shit. Fucking focus you wanker. You can do this.* Maybe, just maybe, if I could make her feel good, she wouldn't notice I had no idea what the hell I was doing.

It was wrong in so many ways, but with the heat surrounding us in a cocoon of lust and need, I didn't care. But more than that, there was something about this woman that made my body hum. There was something dangerous about her. Something about her that called to something in me that had died a long time ago. It was like my body recognized that she was the only one in the world who understood my tune and knew how to make me sing.

For years, I'd avoided sex. The tattoos and the piercings were my way of suppressing the urge and the need. The itching desperation to connect.

Oh, I fucking wanted to, but I couldn't be sure I wouldn't hurt someone. I knew what happened when I lost even the smallest amount of control. And then there was the little problem of seeing what sex did to people. They would kill for it. Imprison another person over it.

Now, I finally understood.

Despite everything I knew, I still needed to know what she felt like. Even if this was nothing but a frenzied fantasy in the middle of a nightmare, for an hour I could pretend that I was normal. I could forget my past and who had forged my existence.

I could fight it all I wanted, but I had to have her. I couldn't help the reverent whispers of her name as I kissed her, touched her, whispered words that stoked the fire between us.

"Gemma—" My voice, thick and gravelly, strained as I kissed down her belly.

"Please, Matthias. I need this. I need you."

My gaze fell on hers as I kissed her soft flesh. "You're so perfect." I sat back and groaned as I rearranged my dick. My eyes never left hers. They narrowed as I sucked in a breath. *Don't fuck this up, mate. You cannot screw this up.*

Gemma sat up on the bed and dragged what was left of the T-shirt over her head. When I mumbled a curse, she smiled.

What she wasn't prepared for was the speed of my response. With a growl, I flattened her on her back underneath me, still careful of her injuries.

When my lips met hers again, my kisses held no patience. No gentleness to coax out her response. I took, plundered, and tasted. I demanded her tongue mate with mine. "Are you sure?"

"Yes," she answered softly. Her hips rose to meet mine and I growled. I tucked a hand under her ass and shoved her hips forward to align with mine. Kissing her, I let my hands roam freely, running them through her hair, over her face, back to her breast. They were so goddamn perfect. I wanted to lick one. Suck one.

When I lowered my mouth to one of the stiff peaks, she threw her head back and moaned.

I could only watch her in awe as heat suffused my body, making my skin tingle. "I didn't know... Complete perfection."

With rough, jerky movements, I dragged her scrub bottoms off and her underwear with them. All thought ceased as I moved my lips down her torso, gently kissing her bruises to her belly button. I pursed my lips and gently blew a heated caress along the top of her mound.

And then my tongue found her slick folds, and I lost any and all tentative hesitation. I devoured her.

Oh. Holy. Hell.

Heaven, she tasted like goddamned heaven. Sweet, like melted sugar on my tongue. I hadn't known it would be like this. There was no way to prepare, to block out the emotion and the intimacy. So instead, I felt it all.

Gemma grabbed two handfuls of my hair and held on. My unrelenting fingers and tongue parted her folds, licking and touching. My thumb traced circles over her clit and she cried out. Then I did the unexpected, running my tongue down her slit to her dewy core, then using my tongue to fuck her.

"Jesus. Oh my God."

"So good," I muttered with a guttural growl. This wasn't enough. This would never be enough.

She answered me with a breathy, "Y-yes, more. Please, more." But the words were strangled in her throat.

I stopped lapping and went back to lazily stroking her clit, teasing her. Shit, at least I hoped that was the clit. I'd had extensive anatomy classes when I was with ORUS, including the anatomy of the female form, in the off chance that I had to use other methods to make someone cooperate.

No. Stop thinking. Be here. With her. She was untouched by my other life and I wanted to keep it that way.

Impatiently, she wiggled against me, and I muttered a curse. She wanted more. And Jesus fuck I wanted to give it to her. But could I have enough control? Would I even know what I was doing?

She raised her hips again. I slid one thick finger inside then nipped at her clit with my teeth. Her orgasm hit her hard, making her legs clamp around my head as she thrashed.

I scooted up her body, keeping up the motions with my finger. My lips pressed to hers again, and I curved my finger until I found the little bundle of nerves inside.

As she bucked beneath me and I swallowed her moans, I couldn't help the rock of my hips against her thigh. As I drove her over the cliff of ecstasy, tingles chased up my spine.

Oh shit. What the fuck was happening?

You're coming dipshit. You know that thing you do in the shower sometimes? This is what it feels like with a girl.

Only about a million times better.

This was supposed to be about her, and I was fucking coming? But it was too late to stop it. Instead I pressed hard against that bundle and dragged another screaming shudder from her. For the time being, she was mine, and I owned every part of her until the dawn stole her away.

———

Gemma

I WASN'T sure how long we stayed like that. Me, naked and limp beneath him, my arms wrapped around his strong back, my nails digging into his flesh. Him, his sweatpants still on, now soaked with my fluids and some of his own.

A part of me knew I should be embarrassed, but I wasn't. Somehow, his big body shielding me from the cold seemed right. It seemed like I was always meant to be beneath him.

What the hell is wrong with you? You don't know this guy. A few days ago he could have killed you. Hell, he almost had. I knew exactly what kind of monster lay inside him, but I didn't care. Not at that moment.

Oh, but he will.

I wasn't sure if he could sense the change in me, but

his breathing changed. The long, easy breaths against the crook of my neck now became a little choppier as if he was trying to control his breathing, trying to stay calm, but freaking out.

Okay, so maybe you should freak out. After all, we'd essentially dry-humped like a couple of teenagers, though it's not like I'd ever done *that* as a teenager. And then he'd gone down on me. Like *really* gone down on me. Like, enjoyed the hell out of himself going down on me.

And, well, yeah, I'd come. So there was that. And now he was freaking out. *As you should be.* But for some reason I wasn't, and I was disappointed that he was. When he drew back, his gaze met mine briefly before skittering away.

"Are you all right?" His voice was low. Growly. Like he'd just spent the last hour doing—well, yeah ... what we'd been doing.

I nodded. "Yeah, I'm fine. I'm just—"

"I'm going to get cleaned up. You should go back to the infirmary."

I frowned. "Wait, what? The infirmary? So you're kicking me out?"

He shook his head and frowned. "No, I just... just give me a second." He ran his hands through his hair and pushed himself up over me before climbing out of the bed. I could only watch his broad back and the way the muscles played as he moved and went to the bathroom. I heard the water running, and he came back with a washcloth. For a moment, I thought he'd hand it to me. But instead, he brushed his fingertips over my belly then tucked the warm, wet cloth against my center. He was efficient about cleaning me but gentle too.

I'd been wet from what he'd done to me, but he also made quick work of wiping away the stickiness on my thigh. And then he turned his back to me and stood. "You're cleaned up now. You should probably get dressed."

The hell I would. "No. What the hell just happened here? You don't want to get in bed?" I hated that sound. The question in my voice, the pleading—that sound came from the Gigi part of me. I wanted nothing to do with Gigi. Gigi was weak. Gigi was scared. Gigi was vulnerable. Gemma was not. Gemma was a fighter. Gemma was impervious to pain. Gemma was a survivor. "I asked you a question. Are you just going to kick me out?"

He'd gone back into the bathroom, and I heard shuffling in there. Then he came back out with the towel wrapped low around his hips.

"Oh my God."

He looked good in his sweats, but he looked even better in a towel.

"It's not that I want you to go. I just... " He frowned. "I just think it's better." He flushed deep crimson and kept his gaze averted from mine.

Oh shit, he was embarrassed. Quickly, I grabbed the scrub bottoms I'd been given, and slid into them. I was only slightly self-conscious about my nudity. Andromeda had taught me early that there might come a day when I had to fight naked. So for the most part, I didn't care. But when I slid my tattered T-shirt back on, I felt like I had a shield.

"Listen, I know that this is maybe awkward or whatever, but I don't know. I felt a connection to you. When I woke up, you were the first face I saw. I don't know what just happened—" I looked at him then back toward the bed. "—or why you wouldn't make love to me, but I'd like it maybe if you held me for a minute."

He frowned. His hands trembled and he braced one of them in the doorway. His knuckles turned white as if he was holding on to keep from coming toward me and touching me. "I don't think that's a good idea."

"Why not? A minute ago, you just told me how beautiful you thought I was. And if that's changed now that you've touched me..." I let my voice trail. Jesus Christ, he was blowing me off. And here I was, begging. This was far worse than when he'd tried to kill me. At least that guy was honest. Direct. Clear. This one, I couldn't read.

"That's not—" He took a deep breath. And then I could see it, as if a mask was going over his face. "Look, love, I'm just not good, okay?"

Somehow, watching him slip the mask on stung more because I thought I could connect to the version of him who at least was open. This version was impenetrable. "Fine, I'll go." I turned to leave, and my gaze found the desk by his bookshelf near the door. In the corner, there was a stuffed toy that was worn and tattered, but there were stitches sewn into one of the little feet. My stomach lurched.

No. No fucking way.

Behind me, I heard shifting. "Gemma look, this is just safer for you. I—"

I whirled on him. "Where did you get that?"

He frowned. "What are you talking about?"

I pointed at the stuffed, worn Tigger toy. Long ago, Matt had stitched it up for me when it had gotten caught on a nail. "*That.* Are you Matt? Are you him?"

11

———————

Matthias

WHAT THE HELL did she just call me?

I glared at Gemma, trying to decipher what and who she was. Was she someone sent by the demons of my past? But the more I stared at her, all I could see was Gigi, around the mouth... the eyes...

Jesus Christ, the eyes. Haunted, soul stripping.

I shook my head. *No. It's not her.* I cleared my throat. "What did you just say?"

She licked her lips, and my gaze couldn't help but track her tongue as it peeked out. Every memory of how she tasted bored its way further into my skull, as if to take root so I could never exorcise her from my brain. My thumb searched my heart against my ribcage, pounding so rapidly it threatened to break free of its cage.

"I called you Matt. Are you him?" Her voice was pleading, questioning, full of disbelief and wonder, and... hope.

She's not her. Gigi's dead. Has been dead for nearly a decade now. This is a trick.

"Who sent you?"

She shook her head. "No. No one *sent* me. Are you Matt?"

"You don't know what the fuck you're talking about." I didn't even bother with pants. I tucked the edges of the towel into each other and went straight for her. Despite the anger coursing through me, somehow the monster inside stayed at bay, happily sleeping, as if sated for the night.

Considering what you just did, you should be.

Fuck. Bugger. I couldn't fucking think of her that way... the way her lips tasted... She was a liar. A spy maybe? I didn't fucking know. All I knew was that I had to get her as far away from me as possible.

The thing was though, even as I bore down on her, she didn't back away. Her gaze never left me. She stood her ground and didn't flinch. Not an inch. Jesus, Mary, and Joseph, the woman had a core of steel. Even the guys in this house would all run for cover if they saw me coming after them like this. She just tucked her chin up and glared at me. "Answer the question."

"You don't know what the hell you're chatting about." I grabbed her by the upper arms and she winced, but I didn't let go. "I don't know who you are, and this isn't a fucking game."

"This isn't a game to me. That stuffed toy... Where did you get it?"

I didn't dare glance in the direction of that stuffed animal. Even Oskar had learned very quickly to never ask me about it. "You belong in the medical bay. Don't come into my room again."

She fought against my hold, but it was futile. "Let me go. Talk to me. I think after what we just did, you owe me that. Where did you get it?"

"We're done talking." I turned her in my arms and practically frog-marched her out of my room, down the hall. She was smart enough to not wake up the others. She was silent until I got her down the hall, made the right toward the main living area and then a sharp turn on the left to the med bay, and then I shoved her inside the room.

But that was where her acquiescence stopped. "Talk to me. Tell me what's going on. Why are you kicking me out? I just want to know if you're him. They told me you were dead. I want to understand." She reached for me and I backed away.

"Whoever you think I am, I'm not him. Whoever you're looking for, I'm sure he's long dead." I wanted to leave her there. I wanted to turn my back, lock her in and shut out the last hour and a half. I was desperate to do that. Desperate to get my emotions back under control, to stop the spinning of the world and just make everything slow down and steady out.

Fucking hell, this wasn't supposed to happen like this. When I raised my eyes, it wasn't Gemma looking back at me. It was Gigi, the only person I'd ever loved in this world who had ever loved me back.

I knew it was a trick. I knew it was a lie. But there was a part of me deep inside, buried somewhere beneath the monster, that wanted to believe—that hoped— even though I knew better. "Stay away from me."

She shook her head and stuttered. "I don't want to hurt you. I just–I just need answers."

"So do I. Let's start with who sent you?" I could practically see the mask sliding in place. She was hiding something. What was it?

"I told you, no one sent me."

"Bollocks. I don't believe you."

She approached me cautiously. "Look, when I was little, I had a Tigger just like that. And there was someone very special who tried to help me. There were bad people that hurt him. They killed him and tried to kill me. That stuffed toy really just looked like mine. It's impossible that you would be him because when I went looking—" She shook her head. "Everyone said he was dead. I even saw what I assumed was his obituary. I thought that I would never see him again, but I just... What if I was wrong? What if they didn't kill him?"

I set my jaw. "Like I said, whoever it is you're looking for, whoever you think I am, I'm not. You need to stay here. Don't come into my room again."

"How can you say that after what happened?"

"What happened was a mistake. It won't be happening again."

She raised her brow. "Are you serious right now?"

I nodded. "As a heart attack. I don't know what your game is. I don't know what you're playing at, but the kind of games you're playing, they get people dead. In case you didn't know it, I am the boogeyman. So even if you're innocent, even if you actually think I am some friend of yours, it's better for everyone if you stay the fuck away. But if you're lying, or if this is a game and someone sent you, for your own safety, you'll want to stay in here until Noah can deal with you. Either way, it means you stay the fuck away from me." And then I did the safest thing that I could. I walked out and locked the door behind me.

———

Matthias

MY LEGS SHOOK.

Oh God, no. No. Even as I drowned out the sound of her thumping on the glass and demanding I let her out, I was having a hard time staying steady on my legs. The swaying and rocking of the penthouse had my stomach lurching.

No. No. No.

The survival instinct cued the monster inside to stretch.

Was it time to fight? Or retreat? It was as if it responded to my call to arms. More like call to puke.

It's not her. Block out the noise. It's not her. Gigi is dead.

I knew what my brain was telling me. The girl with the big eyes, the full lips, and the fire-bright red hair— she was gone. She was never coming back. That's what I told myself. That was what I was forced to believe, forced to accept. As much as I tried to hide it, as much as I tried to swallow it, there was no denying it. No one else in the world would know about that Tigger toy, that doll that Gigi had dragged around behind her in the dirt, the mud, and the rain. As kids, I'd often washed it for her, helping to keep the thing clean.

Shit. Shit. Shit.

I was going to be sick. *It's a lie. It's a lie. It can't be real.* That girl in there was sent by the Family. I'd known that there would be a cost to what I'd been doing, that they would come after me. And they had been. This woman, this Gigi look-alike, she was just the latest in their assault against me.

You knew this would happen.

That's right, I did know. They'd come after my family, and now they were going after the psyche, the tenuous hold I had on my inner killer. They knew who I was and what I was capable of. They were trying to break down my inner sanctum by sending that woman.

Gigi had died. I'd seen her limp body floating along down the Thames. They'd held me back as I tried to jump in after her. The angle with which she'd smacked into the water, there was no way anyone survived that. And, I remembered, Gigi couldn't swim.

So who the hell was that in the medical bay?

The memories of that long-ago night washed over me, racking my body with shivers. Just a few more steps and I'd be in the safety of my room and I could collapse.

It didn't matter what I did though; the memories couldn't be held at bay. It came rushing over me like a tsunami wave.

MATT PEERED AROUND THE GRATE. Becca was back. She looked like she'd gained a pound or two, so wherever she'd been, they were feeding her better. But her eyes, they were dead and flat.

What the hell was she doing here? The Family had sold her a few weeks ago. She was only nine, but still, they'd sold her to someone. Some sick ponce had come to pick her up. Matt's skin crawled thinking about it.

This was the reason his mother had insisted on nurturing his love of all things tech, so that he could avoid having those dead eyes. His stealing of stuff and taking it apart had been a problem for her, but she'd let him. It made him useful in other ways. If Becca was back, that meant the buyer hadn't liked her? What had gone wrong?

Up top, he could see Colin holding her tight, shaking her. Matt's hands furled into fists. He wanted to go up there and beat Colin for touching her. Becca was only a little kid. She didn't deserve that. And then he saw him—Father. The old man was hardly ever seen anymore. Usually only if there was a problem. Matt had only seen him twice, and his mother had always told him, "Stay out of the way, stay hidden, and don't draw attention." She told him that he didn't want the attention of Father.

The older man bent in front of the little girl with the stringy brown hair. He was asking her something. She didn't even respond. No reaction, no emotion, nothing.

Oh yeah, Matt knew that look well. Father and Colin stepped aside to talk privately. And the girl turned her head, their eyes meeting for just a moment. Matt wanted to say something, mouth some words to her to offer some comfort. Anything. But what could he really say? Your life is over? This is the hell we all live in?

He could hear the conversation a little bit between Colin and Father. The buyer who sent her back, he didn't like her. She cried too much and was uncooperative. Besides, she was too old.

Matt's skin crawled. He hated those men, every last one of them. If he could, he would burn the whole place down. He had a plan, a plan to get him and Gigi the hell out of there. He'd been squirreling away some money too, enough for train tickets.

He and his mother came from up north. His gran was up there. If he could find her, they'd have a safe place to go. His mum, she ran away from Gran because Gran said she was unfit to raise him. So one day, in the middle of the night, she'd packed him up and they'd run and ended up in London.

He missed his gran. But if he could get it together, they

could get up there, up north near Newcastle. He remembered the small village, and he was good. All he needed was a computer. If things went well, he could steal one. But right now, his only plan was to get him and Gigi out safely. Maybe another week and they could manage it.

He was good with technology, and he was good at light hacking. He knew all the right people to get the right IDs. And if he was smart and he picked the right wallet, he'd have access to bank accounts, real money... money that little kids couldn't get access to.

Maybe he could take that little girl Becca up there with them. But she'd been sent back. That meant she was safe for now, right? He glanced back up. His eyes scanned the scaffolding and then he saw her to the right. She was climbing up.

The scream lodged in his throat, survival instincts taking over. Don't make a sound, do not be noticed. It's your life or hers. You die, Gigi dies. Becca is on her own.

Still, the part of him that felt compassion, empathy, the part of him that the Family tried to kill, that part wanted to run up to that girl and tell her not to do it. Not to do that terrible thing she was clearly about to do. That there was a way out. That he could save her just like he was going to save Gigi. And then meeting his gaze one more time, she jumped.

The pandemonium was instant. Father and Colin ran for her. The people down below were screaming. Some of the younger girls and the babies cried, and the women cowered. They knew what was going to happen; beatings for everyone. He turned his gaze back to Colin, whose hands were now clutching in his hair. Father shoved at his shoulder and told him to find another girl.

In that moment, Matt knew that they didn't have a week. They needed to leave now.

He didn't think he'd ever run so fast in his life. As small as he was, he shoved past the people in the hallways, the crowds running toward the main area to find out what had happened. He ran against them and found Gigi in her little hidden cubby under the stairs, the one he'd built for her. It had a little shelf under there for her dolls and her little teacups.

"We have to go."

Her eyes went wide. "What? Why?"

"You're not safe. We have to go right now. Pack your things. I'll be right back."

He booked down the hall, down to his mother's room where he slept, to his little padded mattress on the floor. He knew better than to leave anything visible in the room. He'd learned early enough how to sew his mother's outfits together. Every time he'd stolen enough money, he rolled it tight and shoved it into the padding of the mattress and stitched back up the hole. And the next time he had some money, he'd open those stitches up and do it all again. He'd amassed maybe a few hundred quid. It was enough for tickets and food if they had to rough it for a bit.

He tore the mattress open, grabbed the money, and took one of his mother's heavier shawls for Gigi. There was nothing else he wanted. Nothing else he needed. Hell, he had nothing else. When he went back to Gigi, she had her Tigger and a small little backpack with the picture of her father in it along with some coins and some of her teacups in case they wanted to eat or drink anything, she'd said.

He nodded. "Smart thinking. Are you ready?"

She placed her tiny hand in his and smiled up at him. "Yes, let's go."

He didn't even think. He just dragged her behind him along the path he'd already cleared. Mostly everyone was in the main common area of the warehouse. He took her down to the boiler and around an old washing machine. The stupid thing didn't work, but some of the guys figured they could find parts and fix it.

He'd found it with Gareth when they'd been playing hide-and-seek a few months ago, and he'd discovered the tunnel. He knew it was likely a drug running tunnel, but he knew it went to the outside. Unlike Gigi, he was allowed access outside. So once they were on the streets, he knew where to go.

He forced her forward. "Go on. You first."

What he didn't tell her was in case anyone followed

them, at least he could fight and she could still probably make it to the outside. But no one followed. Inch by inch they crawled, getting the dirt from the tunnels in their hair, on their clothes, and on their skin, but freedom wasn't far. He gave her the directions leading her out. And when they reached the break, he helped her open and shove it aside. When he touched her hand, he could feel her shaking.

"All right?" he asked her softly.

She rolled her lips inward and nodded. He could feel the fear in her tiny body, but she was brave. She was a fighter. She was a survivor. They ran out of the alley and down the street. He knew better than to go to the Nick, because the Family had people on the payroll. They wouldn't be helped. They'd be turned right back over. So that wasn't an option.

Besides, he'd already been collared once for pickpocketing. He didn't need that kind of headache, and he hated to think about what would happen to Gigi if he wasn't around.

Finally, they made it along the Thames heading toward Piccadilly Circus. He'd memorized the bus and train sched-ules. If they could just get there, they'd be fine.

Gigi clutched tightly onto his hand. "Matt, are we going to be okay?"

"Yeah, love, I promise. I wouldn't lie to ya."

But that promise was made in vain. It was a promise he couldn't keep. They were so close. The streets got busier as they neared Piccadilly Circus, and he knew that they were almost to safety in the crowds where no one would know them, where they could change clothes, find something to eat, and get on the bus. They could be with his gran in under a day. All he had to do was get them to safety.

But then a hand clamped on his shoulder and he knew. He knew that somewhere along the line he'd made a miscalculation, made a wrong turn. Beside him, Gigi screamed. Someone had her by the shoulders and she was kicking.

"Oy, let her go."

Alan Rice, one of the Family's enforcers, leaned into his face. "Where do you 'fink you're going?"

Matt thrashed, kicked, wiggled, and punched. He was much smaller than Alan, but there was no way he was letting them take Gigi.

"If you weren't so valuable to Father, I'd put an end to this. But he made it clear that we're not going to kill you."

They weren't? Why was he valuable to Father? Yeah, he knew tech, and sometimes he hacked things for the old man at Colin's behest. But he wasn't that useful. Were they going to sell him instead?

"Put me down."

"Happy to oblige," Alan said. When he put him down, Matt realized that they had Gigi and she was fighting.

"Put her down too. It was my idea. I made her do it."

She was crying now. The tears were running down her face. "Matt, no. I came—"

He set his jaw and turned away from her. Maybe if they thought he'd forced her she'd be okay. "I thought I could sell her on my own. Make my own money, run and be free."

Her eyes went wide. "No. Matt, don't—"

Alan laughed. "Oy, looks like we got a businessman on our hands." He leaned closer. "You're valuable to us. Yeah, she's sellable, but Father wants to make a point. You fink we didn't know your plan to run with her? There are spies everywhere, boyo. You two have to learn that."

The other two men that were with Alan were huge to Matt and even bigger when he looked at them in regard to Gigi. They held her higher. At first, he didn't know what they were going to do with her, but then he saw the gleam in their eyes, the joy… and he screamed.

They picked her up and tossed her over the edge.

Matt screamed and fought against Alan's hold as he watched in stricken horror as her little tiny body hit the water. He screamed, and screamed, and screamed, until his voice went hoarse and the licks of fire lit his esophagus. All he saw on the bridge was her doll. The tiny stuffed Tigger she always carried with her.

Finally, Alan let him go and he ran to the bridge. He grabbed the doll and stuffed it under his shirt as he frantically searched the water for her. Maybe, maybe she made it. But he knew the truth. Gigi had confessed to him that she *didn't know how to swim. She was always fascinated with it. She wanted to learn when she got older.*

She was gone because of him. He'd failed her.

I stumbled into my room, crashing on my bed. I clutched at my hair as if I could dislodge the memory. My gaze landed on the expensive scotch Jonas had given me as an early birthday gift. I rarely drank but fuck, I needed to scrub those memories from my psyche.

When they no longer controlled me, I'd be able to think about what to do with that imposter in the medical bay.

12

Gemma

I RATTLED the handle of the infirmary door one more time, as if to remind myself of my predicament. I was locked in, like a kid in time-out.

If anyone I knew ever found out about this, I'd never hear the end of it.

"Ugh! I have to get out of here." I eyed the ceiling, looking for loose ceiling tiles or a vent large enough that I could climb through. But there was nothing. Just racks of medical supplies, a few gurneys, and the lingering smell of antiseptic.

Maybe they'd designed it this way on purpose, but

the medical bay at Blake Security was the perfect impromptu prison.

Distantly, I could hear voices and then laughter. Heat rushed up from my gut. Was he laughing at her? An image of Matthias telling the others about me made me see red. Or Matt. Whoever the fuck he really was.

Could it be him?

I breathed out a long, slow breath at the thought. Against my will, I shuddered with emotion. What if he really was Matt? Memories of warm hugs, shared meals and the certainty of knowing that my pseudo-big brother would take care of me swarmed through my mind. Growing up with the Family had been varying degrees of horrific, but from the moment I'd arrived, Matt had shielded me. His mother had been one of the working girls and he'd grown up in the Family.

Back then, I'd seen him as a welcoming friend, the one safe place in a scary and unfamiliar new one. Now with the benefit of hindsight and maturity, I had a whole new perspective on just how fucked up it was for a kid to grow up there. Matt had taken me under his wing and kept me away from the worst side of that life until the day when he couldn't protect me anymore.

Tears threatened, and I sprang to my feet, horrified at the rare rush of emotion. I was no longer that scared, vulnerable little girl, taken as collateral for my father's bad judgment.

Now I was strong. ORUS-trained and bred through the flames of a life few could have survived. Andromeda had saved me, but she'd been very clear from the start that my survival depended on my ability to adapt and excel. ORUS wasn't a charity, and if I wanted to stay with them, I would have to prove that I deserved to be there.

By being one of their best.

And you did it, I thought bitterly. *Congratulations. You're a star assassin.*

"Motherfucker!" I banged the door with my fist once in frustration.

Distantly, I could hear more laughter, and then one of the voices got closer. I pressed my face against the small window in the door and then jumped back in shock at the sight of two big, green eyes staring back at me.

"Are you okay?" The man peering in was vaguely familiar, so I figured he must have been around earlier.

Hope sparked. Maybe he hadn't gotten word from Matthias that I was supposed to stay in here. If I could convince him that I'd accidentally locked myself in...

I bit my lip, hoping I looked appropriately bashful. "Sorry, I wanted to get a drink of water, but I think I locked myself in."

The man chuckled, and I couldn't help noticing that he was cute in a clean-cut, boy next door sort of way. Like the kind of guy who'd be most comfortable in a sports jersey and a baseball cap. Nice.

"No problem. Just a second."

His face disappeared, and then there were a series of beeps. A moment later, the door popped open.

"Thank you!" I doubled back and grabbed my phone from the nightstand and tucked it into my bra.

If I got an opportunity to leave, I needed to be ready to run. I'd seen all the screens in Matthias's room, so I wouldn't have long before he noticed I wasn't where he'd left me. Hopefully it wouldn't be too hard to get rid of Mr. Nice Guy.

"No problem. I got a message earlier that we had a new client staying on site. My name is Dylan. If you need anything, feel free to ask any of us." His eyes dropped to the bruises visible on my arms, and his lips tightened slightly.

I fought the urge to squirm. Even though my whole plan was for them to think I was a victim, it was still strange to have people looking at me like one. Especially since I knew a hundred ways to kill a man.

I followed him down the hall and around the bend to a bright, open kitchen. Dylan reached into the refrigerator and pulled out a bottle of water, handing it to me before grabbing one for himself. I cracked it open and took a long drink. Damn, I'd actually needed that. Now I just had to figure out how to get rid of the oh-so-helpful Dylan so I could sneak out of here.

"Do you mind if I make a sandwich?" I asked.

He motioned toward the refrigerator. "Feel free. Help yourself."

I opened the fridge and started digging around, hoping that if he saw me busy and occupied he'd go back to whatever he'd been doing before. After a few minutes, Dylan pulled out his phone.

Then he looked up. "Excuse me. I need to check on something."

I grinned to myself and waved absentmindedly over my shoulder. As soon as I heard his footsteps recede, I closed the fridge and ran for the elevator. I hit the button and silently prayed it would come before anyone else came out here. The loud ding as the elevator car reached our floor made me wince, but luckily no one came to investigate. But I didn't let out the breath I was holding until I got in the elevator and the doors closed.

The elevator opened on the ground level, and I walked quickly to the east-side exit. Once I reached the street, I could find a cab. The sooner I got away from this area, the better.

I pulled out my phone and called Ian. He answered after one ring, but I didn't even wait for him to speak.

"Our plan is fucked, and I'm pretty sure I've been made."

His silence was more potent than a loud, angry response would have been. "By who?"

"The target himself!" I hissed.

"The target? How?" Ian sounded incredulous. Then again, why wouldn't he be? ORUS agents were rarely made. Most of them didn't have identities outside of their work, so how could they be?

But most of them didn't have a past like mine, either.

"I know him. The target. He's not just some run-of-the-mill guy. His name is Matthias."

Ian cursed. "What do you mean you know him?"

"In the Family, we were kids there together." I paused. I needed to be careful to stick to the truth as much as possible. ORUS knew I'd grown up in the Family. They knew that I'd run away and that Andromeda recruited me. We'd just fudged the timeline for my running away a little.

"You fucking know him? Why didn't you mention this before I sent you back?"

I sighed. "I didn't realize it was him until tonight. He wasn't pleased. He thinks it's some kind of trick."

"Mother fucker. Abort for now. Come back to the nest. We need to regroup."

He's not your Matt. Despite seeing that toy, there had to be another explanation. But even if there wasn't, his last words to me came back.

Whoever you think I am, I'm not him. Whoever you're looking for, I'm sure he's long dead.

It was a good reminder. Because no matter who Matthias used to be, the only thing that really mattered was who he was *now*.

The enemy.

———

Matthias

IT TURNED out that scotch had a voice.

I lifted my head again as the bottle called out to me with its siren song. The room swam, and I grunted, closing my eyes to ward off the sick swirls. It wasn't so wobbly when I closed my eyes.

"I've never seen him like this." Oskar's voice rumbled over the others', and for once he didn't sound amused. He sounded worried.

"Maybe we should leave the kid alone. Let him lick his wounds in private," Rafe added. He definitely didn't sound worried. Was that disgust?

My thoughts were slowed by the alcohol but I still had enough of my wits to be embarrassed. No doubt the almighty Rafe, ORUS legend, had never humiliated himself by coming on a girl before his dick was even out of his pants only to have the girl sneak away on him. Last night, I'd gone back to the medical bay to talk to Gemma and discovered that she'd given us the slip. It didn't take long to uncover how she'd done it. Dylan hadn't had any reason to assume she was on lockdown. And I definitely wasn't going to tell him what had happened between us.

Shame swept through me like wildfire. These were my guys. The men I counted on to have my back in any situation and men I respected. It had taken years to earn their trust and prove that I was more than just some stupid kid that Noah had saved. Now they were all standing around debating my usefulness and looking at me with pity.

Laughing at me.

"The lot of you can cheerfully fuck off," I mumbled.

All talk ceased, and I felt more than saw them come closer. I tensed. Men coming up behind me wasn't a safe situation. For anyone. All at once I wasn't a fully grown man with years of combat training under my belt. I was thrown back to the years when I was a scrawny preteen with a pretty face and a slim chance at a future.

"People can't be trusted, Matthias. Especially men. It's in their nature to be cruel, to take rather than give. Don't trust 'em."

His mother's voice was soft so that none of the other working girls sitting nearby would hear them. Matthias hated coming to see her here, but Father insisted all the working girls live together. It made them easier to control. At least that's what he'd heard one of the guards say once.

"I won't, Ma. I promise."

She caressed his face, holding his chin between her long, thin fingers. "I wish you didn't look like me. Too pretty for your own good. There are men here who like that. Innocent young boys."

Her face fell, and Matthias threw himself into her arms, pressing his nose against her neck the way he'd always done. He'd never tell her about the things he overheard in the main house now that he'd been handpicked by Father to train as one of his guards. Matthias had always been good with numbers and could remember most anything he learned in school, even if he only heard it once. Father himself had come to see him after school at the warehouse one day and told him that his grades would take him places. That he was proud.

He'd gone to live in the main house that day, even though

he'd hated to leave Mama behind. But she'd told him it was for the best. Now that Matthias was a little older, he understood why.

There were things that children should never see. For example, he'd never forget the sight of Father leaving his Mama's room that afternoon.

I groaned and tried to open my eyes again. It was like unrolling a wet carpet.

"Well, what do you know? It's alive!" Oskar kneeled down to peer in my face.

If I could have lifted my arm I would have popped the wanker right in the face. As it was, I could barely get out a mumbled "fuck off" without slurring.

I'd probably overdone it a bit with the scotch. If I hadn't been recruited by ORUS, no doubt I would have used alcohol to numb the pain, to anaesthetize myself against the memories that tormented me. But my training had been too intense, and I couldn't afford to have my senses dulled in any way. We'd all been drilled to believe that the body was our finest weapon and to abuse it was to waste a valuable resource. So I'd never touched alcohol.

Until tonight. Until I'd fucked things up with Gemma. Or was she Gigi? Fuck, I didn't know. But I'd never forget the look on her face when she saw that stuffed toy.

"I'm so sorry, Tigger. I fucked this up." I moaned again as my head burst with pain. I'd always thought you weren't supposed to have a hangover until the next morning. But I felt like fresh roadkill already.

Just how long had I been in here drinking anyway? I had to find Gemma, find out who she was.

"I'm coming, Tigger," I mumbled.

A large hand settled on my shoulder, startling me so badly it felt like my heart stopped beating. When I opened my eyes, Oskar was peering at me, his blue eyes so bright they were almost blinding.

"Jesus, it's even worse than I thought," Oskar declared. "He's talking about stuffed animals."

13

———

Matthias

"WHAT THE FUCK is wrong with him?"

Next to me on the couch Oskar shrugged. It required herculean effort for me to crane my head in Oskar's direction. It required even more effort to keep my head straight. All the damn thing wanted to do was fall back. It was as if my skeleton was too tired to hold it up.

Or you just consumed a baby elephant's-worth of scotch.

I hadn't had that much to drink, had I?

Oskar shook his head. "I don't know. I think he might be a furry."

I tried to make my mouth move, to form words even,

but to no avail. I just ended up sitting there with my mouth open and my damn tongue not functional. *It was functional yesterday, wasn't it?* God damn it. I did not need to get a boner around these guys. There would be laughs and comments. So. Many. Comments.

It was bad enough I'd humiliated myself with Gemma. It was worse that I hadn't seen she was an obvious plant, and then... God, I fucked up the whole sex thing which was just... I knew the spy thing was bad. But somehow the sex thing—that *felt* worse.

I dragged my head up again to glare at them all. But I couldn't get my damn eyeballs to move properly.

"What the fuck is a furry?" Rafe demanded.

The German made this chuffing noise. It was as close as the guy ever got to a laugh. "Look man, don't ask me that. You don't want to know."

Rafe laughed. "Now I gotta know. What is it, and why do you think the kid here is one of them?"

Oskar pulled out his phone, typed something quickly and handed it over to Rafe. "Well, the kid has been going on and on about Tigger, so I assumed he was talking about *Winnie the Pooh*. You know, Tigger. Bounce, bounce, and all that good shit?"

I tried to make sense of the conversation that was happening around me, but I couldn't. My brain was too foggy. My muscles were a mess and unable to function.

You know better than this. This is deadly.

Yes, but I was home. Oskar could handle himself, and Rafe was ready, so if someone did break in here, likely they'd be dead before they even made it past the foyer. Not to mention I'd put in kick-ass security protocols.

Did you forget they were bypassed just a few days ago? Next to me on the other side of the couch, Rafe groaned. "You've got to be kidding me."

Oskar chuckled again before taking his phone back. "I shit you not. That's a furry."

Rafe sat forward and rubbed the heels of his palms into his eyes. "I can't fucking unsee that. I mean, I have questions though. How does that work exactly? It's not like their parts work."

Oskar shrugged. Matthias could feel the simple action as his friend's shoulders slipped up and down on the fabric of the couch. "I don't fucking know. I'm not an expert or anything. It's not like I was saying I'm into that; I'm saying the kid is."

Wait, what? What the hell were they talking about?

Rafe shook his head. "I've never seen him dressed up. And no judgment here but that goes beyond the kid's realm of weird."

Noah appeared in the doorway. "What's up? What are we talking about?"

Oskar was ever so helpful. "Rafe wanted to know what a furry was, so I enlightened him. And Matthias is one. Also, he's toasted."

Noah frowned. "Kid, you been drinking?"

I found it funny that was the statement Noah found alarming. "Yep."

My friend and mentor frowned. "Want to tell us why?"

"Fucking felt like it, mate." I frowned. I shouldn't have said that. Noah had a right to worry. I rarely ever drank. Being drunk meant I had lower inhibitions... and far less control over the more violent nature of my character.

Noah's brows lifted, but he said nothing.

If Oskar noticed his shitty attitude, he said nothing. He was still on the furry thing. "We were just trying to figure out a viable reason for Matthias to walk in here mumbling on and on about Tigger or something. Rafe says no way, but my money says the lad is a furry."

Rafe shuddered. "Look man, I can't unsee that shit. The imagery is burned into my skull now."

Oskar flashed Rafe a grin. For a moment I blinked. Oskar never smiled. Why the hell was he flashing a grin at Rafe? "I figured if I had to have this knowledge, then so should you. Besides, it's not me that brought it up. It was the kid talking about Tigger. I don't even know what that means. Maybe it's some kind of, like, furry sub-species. I don't know. But he's been on about it for the last twenty minutes."

I finally realized what the hell they were talking about; sex, and the people who got off on wearing the cosplay of furry animals and then rubbing themselves all over each other. I wasn't one to judge. After all, look at the fucked up pile of steaming goop that was my life. Whatever people wanted to do to get off, I didn't care. Except they were suggesting that I was one of them.

I frowned. "Wait, I'm not a furry." Oskar tapped me on my left shoulder, and I had to physically fight to not lean into Oskar's bigger body. "Are you fucking laughing at me, mate?"

Oskar nodded. "Yep. You deserve it. Who told you to go and get fucked up anyway? Leaving us out of the fun?"

I shook his head. "I needed a drink. After what I fucked up, I needed to drink. I had a bottle, opened it, and started drinking."

"Just how much have you had to drink?" asked Noah.

I forced my body forward, nearly catapulting myself off the couch, and grasped the empty scotch bottle on the floor next to me. "I had this."

Oskar nodded. "That was some prime scotch, man." He shrugged. "You are going to have a hell of a hangover tomorrow morning, kid. What's so bad that you had to crack open your birthday present early?"

I shook my head. There was no way I was talking about this. "No. I know you. You're going to take the piss. I can hear it now. I mean, look at you. I need help, and you lot are laughing at me? Fuck the lot of you."

Rafe chuckled low. "Right, kid. Something going on? Like Noah said, it's not like you to drink. Not on a school night and all."

"I fucked up. That's what happened. I fucked up, and I couldn't help but touch her, and I just fucked the whole thing up." I knew I sounded sloppy. I could hear my swords slurring. Bugger.

Rafe gave me a bemused look, and somehow that did not make me feel calm in any way. "Okay, relax. What the happened? With who?"

"Her... the girl we brought in yesterday, or rather, who brought herself in. She climbed into my bed and you know..."

From my left Oskar offered, "Did she touch you in your special place, Matthias?"

I might have been wasted, but I knew enough to throw a punch that landed in Oskar's direction. It only slightly connected, but it was good enough to make me feel better. And what do you know? That settled my stomach right down. There was nothing like a little violence to settle the stomach. Better than ginger oil and crackers.

"Stop it." Noah's command was low, tight, and brooked no arguments.

Oskar grumbled. "The fucking kid hit me. I'm not supposed to hit him back?"

Noah gave me a shake of the head. "No. Matthias is pretty wasted, so we don't have any precautions if there is a fight. Do the three of you hear me?"

I scowled. "Stop talking about me like I'm not here. I told you, I fucked everything up."

Rafe's voice was soothing. "Kid, what are you talking about? You're saying the girl that came in here with the bruises on her climbed into your bed?"

I nodded. "Yup, in my room. I figured she was lost, but nope. She said we had a connection or something. But the point is I fucked it up. I don't even know what to do during sex."

On my left, Oskar sat slack-jawed. "What?"

I couldn't even bother to answer him directly. "It was going so good and it felt... and I wanted... but then, I realized I didn't know what the fuck I was doing. So I just went—but that was stupid because I didn't do it right."

Rafe held up his hands. "Wait. Okay, I'm trying to get my head wrapped around this. The girl from yesterday coming into your bed... you know, whatever. There's no accounting for taste. But how do you get to the *almost having sex and fucking that up* part?"

I was fighting to keep the truth inside. But apparently, liquor loosened my tongue. "I went down on her, and I'm pretty sure I did it wrong."

Oskar snorted. "You can't do it wrong. Did she come?"

I frowned. "I don't know. I think so. There was shaking, and she was wet... really, really wet."

Rafe and Noah stared at him. "What do you mean you don't know if you did it right? I mean, she seemed to be having fun, right?" Rafe asked.

I frowned. "I think so. I d-don't know. Fuck, my head. I think I need to start drinking coffee. Pissed isn't really working for me."

"I agree with that. How is it you don't know what to do during sex? It's not like you're a virgin," Noah said incredulously.

This was the part where I could shut everything down, back away very slowly and pretend this conversation never happened. Unfortunately, my legs didn't fucking work. And as a matter of point, neither did my fucking arms. But, joy of joys, my tongue was working just fine. "I am. I've never had sex. So I guess that's technically a virgin."

Rafe guffawed. "The hell you haven't."

I shook my head. Back and forth. Back and forth. The motion made my head swim. Okay, no more shaking of the head. "Nope, not I, said the fly. And I still haven't fucked because I screwed that up." I chuckled. "That rhymes. And then I kicked her out of bed because she's a spy." I whispered that last part, but somehow it sounded so loud in my head.

Rafe's brows were down. "What do you mean, a spy?"

I leaned over. Ooops. Shit... *too far. Too far.* My whole upper body fell on top of Rafe, and he shoved me back up into a sitting position. "She is, mate. Yeah, she's a spy. She was sent to fuck with me." I nodded sagely. Yup, she was. I knew it, and now my brothers knew it too. "She was sent here by the Family. She's pretending, and she tasted so good, and I really, really wanted to fuck her. But not in a sleazy way... I just really needed her, you know?"

Rafe blinked. Okay, it was not the response I was asking for. He turned to Oskar for solidarity. The blond German still sat there staring at me. Noah. Noah would offer sage advice. But nope, he was also doing the open-mouthed guppy thing.

"Oi, what the fuck is the matter with you three?"

Rafe snapped out of it first. "You're a fucking virgin?"

"Shit. Did I stutter? Yeah, I've never had sex. Where I grew up, sex was the devil. So now I don't know what to do. God." I leaned toward Rafe again, and this time Rafe put a hand on my shoulder to keep me upright. "Do you think she's the devil? She must be. That's why the Family sent her for me, because they knew I'm one of the demons from hell. They sent her to claim me."

Finally, Oskar snapped out of it and let out an explosive guffaw. "Look, you're blasted, so we'll wait for you to sober up to ask about this spy nonsense. But can we get back to the important shit? You're a fucking virgin?"

I scowled. "Shout it from the rooftops, why don't you? You're supposed to be helping me. I thought you guys were my brothers."

Rafe nodded. "Yeah, we are. And that's why we're going to give you shit for this."

Matthias

Rafe and Noah exchanged glances.

"Okay, so what happened?" Rafe's voice was calm, reassuring. I glanced at him. Lately, something had changed between us. Rafe wasn't so contentious, and I wanted to kill him less and less every day. So yay for progress.

"With the girl?"

Rafe nodded. "Yeah, keep it simple. Leave out the Tigger and other random-spy shit. We'll figure that out when you're sober, because right now you're not making any fucking sense."

I frowned. Yes, that part I could do. The rest of it—I was still trying to force my brain into analytical mode to assess it all, to try and find the truth of what was going on. But maybe that truth was better kept hidden, at least for the time being. "Okay, so I saw her in medical bay, and I don't know... There was just something about her. You know. Like she's innocent, right?"

Rafe nodded. A slight smirk touched his lips. "Yeah, been there."

I nodded. "You know, I couldn't help it. I just wanted to be near her. I don't understand."

Oskar made that chuffing sound again. "It's okay. I'll explain all the things to you. When a boy likes a girl, sometimes his body reacts." The German said it slowly as if I were deaf and dumb.

"Fuck off, you wanker. I've probably seen more sex in my life than you have. It's what happens when your mom is a slag." *Shit. Stop fucking talking. Right now.* The monster jerked against his chains as if he were trying to claw his way into my brain to take over the controls. *Loose lips get people killed, asshole.*

Oskar frowned. "What?"

I shook my head and turned my attention back to Rafe. "Yeah, so... I like her. I don't know why. It's not like I know her. But she seemed good, like she didn't deserve what happened to her." Little had I known that she was the ghost of my past who came to haunt me. "I just wanted to be near her, I guess."

Rafe nodded. "Yeah, okay, what happened next?"

"I don't know. Later that night, I was in bed. You know, trying to sleep. Not that that happens often. I was mostly just waiting for another proximity alarm."

Rafe's brow snapped down. "Why were you waiting for another proximity alarm? I thought the hack was random?"

There I went with my mouth again. *Lock it down boy. You're going to get caught.* "It was, but I have to be ready just in case."

Rafe nodded. "Okay, what next?"

I could feel my skin flushing and heating, the crimson running up my neck through my veins, making my face feel hot and flushed. "She knocked on my door. I thought it was one of you, so I just told her to come in. God, she looked so tiny, you know, like she needed protection? She said she didn't want to be alone and I—"

"The little soldier stood at attention?" Oskar offered helpfully.

"Shut it. I don't know what happened. She climbed into bed next to me and wanted to cuddle. I'm not exactly a cuddler."

Rafe's chuckle was low. "You don't say."

"I didn't mean to touch her. I didn't. But she just felt so good and then she kissed me." I raised my gaze to meet Rafe's. "What the fuck is that about? Who in their right mind kisses me?"

There was something in Rafe's expression that went soft. Was that pity? No one ever pitied me. I didn't need pity. I wasn't someone to be pitied. I was something to be feared.

"And anyway, I fought. I think I did, anyway. Then she kissed me again and then the next time she kissed me, I just—I don't know. Something snapped. Next thing I knew she was ripping off my shirt, mate. And I got her clothes off and... God, she has the best fucking nipples."

Rafe put up a hand. "Okay, fair enough, yes. The hot girl had great nipples. I hear you so stop shouting."

I frowned. "I'm not shouting."

Rafe chuckled. "Yes, you are."

I tried to modulate my voice. "Yeah, all right, mate. Anyway, she tasted so good. I mean, why do they taste so good? Is that what all women taste like?"

Rafe smiled. "No, they don't all taste that good."

I frowned. "How am I supposed to know who tastes good and who doesn't?" I didn't realize I'd asked it out loud until Rafe chuckled.

"You just find the one that tastes good *to you*."

I frowned but nodded. Gemma tasted good to me. *No, you nitwit. She is a spy. Remember? She's pretending to be Gigi.* Yes, Gigi. The girl he'd loved. But still, as his brain tried to make the connection, he didn't see it. She wasn't Gigi. *But even if she's not... even if she's just there to fuck with you, she sure did taste good.* Wasn't that the truth?

Rafe snapped his fingers in front of my face.

"Come on, what next?"

"Uh, I don't know. We were kissing, and I was just licking, and sucking, and—"

Oskar groaned. "I can't keep this up. I'm gonna get a boner."

Rafe muttered under his breath. "It doesn't take much for you."

I spoke again. "And I went down on her."

Rafe frowned. "Okay, this is the part that's important. Did she like it?"

I frowned. "Yeah." I remembered the way she bucked against me, holding my head in position, raising her hips to meet my tongue. Moaning. Begging. Her little whispers of, *'Please don't stop. Please don't stop. Please don't fucking stop.'* I cleared my throat. "Yeah. She liked it."

Oskar offered up an indelicate question. "What my man here is trying to ask you is did she get off or not?"

"Yeah, I think so."

Rafe sighed. "Okay, maybe that's beside the point. So the whole problem is that you have no idea what to do?"

I shook my head. "No, no. After all the thrashing, moaning, I mean, I've seen enough porn to know *what* to do, but I was afraid of hurting her. And I've never done it before, so I didn't want to fuck it all up, you know."

Rafe nodded. "Okay, so basically, you want to figure out the whole sex thing, without the commentary." He threw Oskar a knowing look.

Oskar held up his hands. "What did I do?"

Rafe sighed. "Okay, look, we can help. There's this place."

I frowned. "No, no hookers." I swallowed hard. "It's just not happening."

Rafe's eyes went wide as his brows popped. "No, it's not like that. It's a sex club. No one's gonna touch you.

You don't have to touch anyone, but you will learn a thing or two."

Oskar sat up straight. "First, I want to know why Assassin Boy here knows about this place and I don't. And second of all, no one's leaving me behind. When do we leave for this little field trip?"

Noah pushed away from the wall. "I'm glad you two have this in hand. Lucia would kill me if I went anywhere like that. You know how she gets."

Rafe laughed. "You mean you know how you get. Lucia will be curious. Anyone who looks at her wrong, hell, you're going to leave a trail of bodies. And then we won't be invited back, so you're clearly not allowed to come to the club."

At that moment, Diana walked in. "Did someone say we're going to a club? I want to go."

Rafe dropped his head into his hands. "Babe, no. It's not that kind of club."

She shrugged. "I don't care what kind of club it is. I want to come."

He lifted his gaze to hers. "Like Noah, I probably won't be held responsible for what I do if someone touches you at a sex club."

"Oh, I *really* want to go now. I've always wanted to go to one."

Rafe rolled his eyes to the heavens, and for once I

felt the tension in my shoulders ease. It was rare to see Rafe flustered.

"Fine, you can come. Kid, are you in?"

Even though there was a part of me that didn't completely trust Gemma, at some point I would need some practical-application knowledge, and maybe the club was just the right place to go. "Yeah, I guess I'm in, mate."

14

Gemma

I LOOKED up at the sound of the door opening. This safe house belonged to ORUS so there was little chance anyone was breaking in, but years of training left me on guard for anything. When Ian's face appeared in the doorway, I relaxed but only slightly.

He didn't look pleased. Sure enough, he started in with the questions right away.

"Okay, explain what happened yesterday. How are you so sure you were made?"

I clutched my arms, suddenly cold as ice. Matthias's face appeared in my mind. He'd been so vibrant one moment, devouring my mouth like it held the nectar of the gods, and then completely vacant the next. I could have been a complete stranger with the way he'd looked at me.

Maybe that was how he was. The Matt from my childhood hadn't been like that, so the toy had to be a coincidence. He'd probably gotten it from an ex-girl-friend who'd dumped him or something. It could explain why he'd gotten so pissy that I'd asked about it. But even as I had the thought, I knew. I *knew* it was the same toy I'd fallen asleep with each night as a child. That thing had once been my life and just as precious to me as a real sibling. When I'd woken after being fished out of the Thames that night, I'd mourned for it so long that Andromeda had been concerned for me.

"Matthias. He kept insisting I was a spy," I said.

Ian moved around the couch and perched on the arm, all the while watching me carefully. "Now how exactly did you know him? The guy is a ghost. Untouchable."

"He saved my life once. I thought he'd died as a result. But I guess he just became ORUS."

Ian appeared to be speechless.

"Everyone comes from somewhere. Even ghosts. I should know." I smiled grimly, thinking of all the tech wizardry Andromeda must have had to pull off to invent a new identity for a random girl she found floating in the river one night. But somehow she'd done it. She'd taken me to America and created a whole new identity for me as Gemma Boyd.

"That's true but this kid is different. You have to understand the stories floating around about him. He's ORUS legend now, just as much for how he left ORUS as for how he joined. We might be able to use your connection to get you back in."

"That's madness, and you know it." I settled back on the couch, sinking into the cushions. ORUS safe houses weren't flashy for obvious reasons, but they were always comfortable and well-tended inside. They took care of their weapons, I thought bitterly. Suddenly I was more interested than ever in how Matthias had managed to escape.

"How did he get out of ORUS?"

Ian crossed his arms. "This was about five years ago. The timeline is a little uncertain. I wasn't Orion then, obviously. Just another agent working my way up the ranks. There were a few agents that were rising fast, and everyone had their eye on them: Leo and Perseus." He glanced over at me.

I thought back. He'd taken his shirt off in front of me, but I'd been far more interested in the ink covering his chest than looking for ORUS markings at the time.

My face flamed with the knowledge. Luckily Ian was too absorbed in his story to notice.

"Anyway, Perseus was known as Orion's personal hacker. It was unheard of for an agent so young to get anywhere near the big boss. Others in the agency weren't happy about it, but no one could touch that kid when it came to skill level. If anyone had dared to challenge him, he could have wiped their entire existence away just as easily as erasing a chalkboard. No one wanted to fuck with that kid."

I shook my head. "He seems so unassuming in person. You'd never know how deadly he can be."

Ian gave her a wry look. "Don't we all? The kid was training with one of the best agents at that time. Leo is now known as Noah Blake. Noah was trained by Libra, also known as Rafe DeMarco."

I sat up fast. "Holy shit! Rafe DeMarco is Libra? The one I've heard all the stories about?"

Ian chuckled. "The one and only."

"So what do they have to do with Matthias? They're a little older so they wouldn't have been in his training class, right?"

"No. But Leo took Perseus under his wing after the kid got him out of some scrape or another. Trained him in hand-to-hand and kept him away from the others.

Protected him as he grew and his skills increased. No matter how well-trained, Perseus was still a teenager at that time. If some of the other agents had wanted to take him out, they probably could have. A teen boy against grown men? It could have been bad, but Leo kept him safe."

It was hardly the point of the story, but I couldn't stop thinking about Matthias being at the mercy of older, hardened agents. I owed Noah Blake a debt of gratitude for playing the big brother when Matthias needed one.

"One day, there was all this chatter about how Leo had requested a meeting with Orion. Back in those days, you didn't just request a meeting with the leader lightly. The old Orion was a paranoid son of a bitch and usually kept his location a secret. But the next day we all found out that Leo and Perseus were gone; out of ORUS and their status changed to Deactivated."

"Deactivated?" I wrinkled my nose. "I've never even seen that status before."

"Exactly." Ian's eyes gleamed. "That's because the only two statuses ORUS used for decades were Active and Terminated. No one got out. Not unless they were in a body bag."

Suddenly he got serious, his facial expression hardening. Ian leaned forward, his eyes holding hers. "It's much the same with the Family. But then again, I think you already know that."

I was suddenly so tired. "What do I do?"

"If we can get you back in, you have to complete this mission. Do you understand? Bringing Perseus to us is the only way you can save him. The Family won't stop until they think he's dead."

There was a fervor in his voice that made me uncomfortable. I had to wonder whether Ian had more riding on this mission than he'd told me. Or if there was more going on than it appeared.

He stood and walked into the attached kitchen. I heard the water running in the sink and the sound of the refrigerator opening. Normal, everyday sounds playing in the background as I thought of how to save two lives. Sabine was counting on me but I couldn't betray Matthias either.

Finally, I raised my head to see Ian watching me from across the room. It wasn't pity on his face. I doubted he was still capable of experiencing that emotion, or any emotion at all. But he did look disturbed.

"This girl must be some friend." He said it like the notion of having a friend was unfamiliar.

"I made her a promise. I can't just leave her. I need to get to Father."

Ian's lips tightened. "Do you think Matthias knows who you work for?"

I shook my head. "I think he was just in shock that it was me. He kept saying 'who sent you?' but if he'd really thought I was on a mission, I doubt he'd have left me there without alerting anyone else."

"Well then, your cover hasn't actually been blown, has it? As far as he knows, you're just an old friend come out of the blue. Coincidences happen. Make it count."

I thought of how my life had come full circle. Snatched from my bed as a child by monsters, protected by a boy who owed me nothing. Now the only thing standing between me and saving my friend was the boy I owed my life to. "There's no such thing as coincidence."

Ian shrugged. "Maybe not. But you're here and possibly the only one who can get through to him. Go back in. You could be saving his life by bringing him back into ORUS."

I stood. "I doubt he'll see it that way." It was already a bitter pill; imagining the look on Matthias's face when he realized I'd double-crossed him.

"Does it matter? He'll be alive. We're the only ones who can really protect him. And then he can help us get Father."

I only hoped that he'd one day understand what I'd

done. Because losing him twice in one lifetime wasn't something I could survive.

———

Matthias

I TOOK a small sip of coffee, grimacing at the taste. I usually took my coffee black, but this was on another level, like death in a cup. But at least I was more alert.

I was inside a sex club and I was pretty sure I didn't want to be here. I'd seen plenty of sex. But Rafe had insisted what I had seen growing up had been about power, control and abuse. He'd said what happened here was about nothing but pleasure.

There was a part of me that wanted to bail, to run, to block it out. There was another part of me that was sure I'd be numb, like always and not feel anything.

And then there was the part of me that was...curious. I wanted to see if what I'd felt with Gemma was a feeling I could conjure up anywhere else. I wanted to know if it was possible I wasn't completely dead inside. If the desire wasn't a fluke.

Also...if it wasn't a fluke, maybe I needed to learn what the fuck I was doing.

"I can't believe people actually do this stuff. And that

they don't mind people watching." I glanced to my left. I was sitting in a booth on the main floor of the club. Narrow walkways wound between the booths so the girls dancing on the main stage could come closer and perform if they wanted.

A brunette with wild, dark curls sashayed down the walkway next to my booth, pausing to bend over and touch her toes, peeking at me from between her legs. I choked on the sip of coffee I'd just taken, gasping as some of it went up my nose. Rafe patted me on the back, but his hand was so heavy it felt like I was being beaten.

I sucked in a breath and held up my hand to ward off any more 'helpful' blows from Rafe. "I'm good, mate. Thanks."

Rafe chuckled. "I think she's flirting with you."

I looked over and watched as the brunette wrapped herself around the pole at the edge of the stage and then did an inverted move so that she could watch me upside down as she spun around the pole.

I could feel myself blushing from head to toe. "She'd just be disappointed."

Rafe leaned forward, and my fingers curled around the coffee I'd been nursing for the past hour. "I know it looks intimidating. But sex is about a lot more than body parts."

"I bet knowing how to work the parts helps though,

huh?" I thought about my humiliating experience with Gemma and sighed. I didn't even know how to keep control long enough to actually have sex. I'd come too fast, before we'd even gotten anywhere.

Rafe chuckled. "Believe it or not kid, knowing the anatomy is the easy part. Hell, with your brain we could just have you memorize a fucking medical textbook overnight and you'd be good to go on that."

I decided not to mention that I'd already read the standard textbooks used at Harvard Medical School a few years ago.

"But the mechanics aren't where most guys go wrong. It's the emotions. The connection. For years, I slept with random women; most had no clue who I really was. I thought that was the safest thing. No one could get hurt. But sex with someone after you actually give a fuck is way better." Rafe took a sip of his drink and then checked his watch. "Actually, we should move this along a little."

I was disappointed. We hadn't been here very long. Rafe's fiancée had come with us but very thoughtfully left us alone to talk. I appreciated that. It was humiliating enough to talk about this stuff in front of the guys. But if I had a girl waiting who looked at me the way Diana looked at Rafe, I wouldn't want to waste my night taking some sex-illiterate kid around a sex club either.

"It's okay, mate. We can go."

"We're not going anywhere except into the public viewing area. You thought I was ditching you that fast?"

I glanced behind us. "Isn't Diana waiting for you?"

Rafe chuckled. "Believe me she's enjoying herself right now. Probably too much."

"Still, I'm sure you have better things to do," I trailed off miserably.

Rafe raised his eyebrows. "And I thought I had trust issues. Come on." He slapped some money on the table and then motioned with his head for me to follow.

We slid out of the booth and then walked next to the stage as we crossed the room. I had the urge to lower my eyes, as if I were being disrespectful to ogle them, but then I remembered this was why we were here. They wanted to be seen. It was oddly freeing.

The girl I'd seen earlier wiggled her fingers at me as we passed, and I smiled nervously. She was gorgeous with small, petite features and full, bouncy breasts that moved tantalizingly as she walked. But she also reminded me of Lucia a bit, which made me feel disloyal immediately. So I kept walking.

Another girl danced at the end of the stage, and her almost-black hair and long, lithe body immediately made me think of Gemma. And what do you know?

Hello instant boner.

"Jesus," I whispered, walking faster until we were out of the main lounge area and in a dark hallway.

"These are the public viewing rooms," Rafe said, motioning to the various windows that were visible. "They know they're being watched. They get off on it. Each window has something different. Take a look. I'll be out front getting another drink while you... browse." He smirked and then walked off.

I was intensely thankful that I'd been left alone for this part. I definitely didn't need another bloke with me as I watched this stuff. It was embarrassing enough.

I approached the first window cautiously. Based on what I'd passed just coming in, anything could be waiting behind that glass. When it became obvious what the people, the many people, behind the glass were doing, I backed away slowly. It was intimidating enough to watch two people having sex; I wasn't ready to watch an entire group going at it.

I shook my head and then walked on. The next room was decorated to look like a doctor's office. A man wearing a white coat had a woman bent over a gurney, plowing into her from behind. From her soft whimpers, he wasn't being gentle about it either. My protective instincts raised up. It was difficult for me to watch any woman in distress, but Rafe had stressed to me before we entered that everyone in this club was screened carefully and was engaging in consensual play. As I watched closer, the woman's face broke into a smile of satisfaction as she shivered in delight.

Okay, so she was enjoying herself. It might not be to my taste but as long as they were both cool with it. I walked to the next window. Each one was decorated to mimic a particular fantasy. There was a police interrogation room, an office with a desk and printer, and even a kitchen. Did people have chef fantasies? It was all a bit strange to me; mildly arousing, but strange. Was this what women liked? Games and fantasy?

Then I walked to the last window. For a moment, I was confused. Most of the other rooms had been decorated so carefully but this one was just done like a standard bedroom. It was dark, save for the golden light spilling from the lamp on the night table. A couple writhed on the bed.

The man was holding the woman down and licking between her legs as she moaned lustily.

I paused, every cell in my body instantly on fire.

My eyes tracked how the man touched her, his hands running over her thighs and calves gently as he pleasured her with his mouth. Every few seconds, he glanced up at her as if checking on her welfare, and the woman tangled her hands in his hair, encouraging him with soft caresses.

God, the way they looked at each other. I could feel the love between them even from outside the room.

Instantly, I stepped back. Even though these rooms were for public viewing, what was going on in there seemed too intimate, too precious to be shared with just anyone. But like a moth to flame, I was drawn back to the window when I saw the man move back, wiping his mouth on the bed linens before kissing up the slight curve of the woman's belly and then over her breasts. She wasn't as big up top as the girls on the stage, but the man didn't seem to care. His big hands cupped her breasts gently, lavishing kisses on both before he settled on top of her.

With a happy giggle, the woman accepted his weight, wrapping her legs around his waist, tilting her face up for a kiss. I practically had my nose to the glass, desperate to see what happened next. The woman looked so happy, so loved. This man clearly knew what he was doing.

As they kissed, their lips never separating for even a moment, the man lifted up and reached between them. By the way his arm moved I figured he was stroking her clitoris. I knew that much from all my reading. Sure enough, the woman only broke the kiss to scream in pleasure. Then the man lowered himself and thrust hard.

I spun around, my heart beating fast, my dick hard enough to drive nails with. Walking quickly, I passed all the other windows until I emerged into the main lounge again, the noise and music hitting me from all angles after the quiet intimacy I'd just witnessed.

Then I skidded to a halt.

Rafe was sitting in the same booth with Diana straddling his lap. Her long, blond hair flowed over her back as she kissed him, the way their bodies rocked indicating what was happening below the table.

Shit. I thrust a hand through my hair. I definitely didn't want to interrupt, but I wasn't sure I could handle walking down the hall of fantasies again either. In theory, it sounded like a good idea, bring the virgin kid to a sex club and show him how it's done. But in a way it was like taking a diabetic to a candy shop. I could watch other people make love a million different ways and still be just as lost in the weeds.

Because I had no idea how to get from point A to where Rafe and Diana were currently wrapped around each other. And that was what I wanted.

Rafe finally noticed me standing awkwardly in the middle of the lounge. He patted Diana affectionately on the rump and murmured something that made her go stiff as a board.

Despite all the naked girls dancing a few feet away,

Rafe's eyes never strayed from Diana. The sight made me chuckle. That was surely love. The man was surrounded by naked, sexy women and all he was interested in was the woman on his lap.

"All right, kid?" Oskar appeared at my elbow. His blond hair was askew and he looked like he'd buttoned his shirt in a hurry.

"Where were...?" I realized that was probably the wrong question to ask in the middle of a sex club. "Uh, hey. Ready to go?"

"In a bit. I see Rafe is still wrapped around his future ball and chain." Oskar winced. "Better him than me. I'm never letting a chick tie me down. Let me go settle the bill."

I grunted an acknowledgement, but my thoughts went back to the couple in the dark bedroom.

If that was what it meant to be chained, I'd welcome being tied down.

I screwed up with Gemma, and I needed to track her down. If for nothing else than to get some answers. And I had to figure out practical application, but I wasn't going to learn that here. First things first: find Gemma. And given how things had ended, that might be easier said than done.

15
____

Matthias

The ride back to the penthouse was awkward. Rafe and Diana were practically clawing all over each other. It was one of the few times Rafe had used a driver, so I chose to ride shotgun instead of being stuck in the back with those two.

To be fair, they weren't nearly as bad as Noah and Lucia, but I knew exactly what they'd be getting up to the moment they hit the penthouse. Oskar, surprise, surprise, had chosen to stay, which was... whatever.

I, on the other hand, needed to go to bed. I was feeling edgy and needed to process everything that had happened over the past day.

A good night's sleep would do wonders. *That's if you think you can sleep.*

The car dropped us at the corner so we could go in the front. The driver would take the car down to the garage, park it and leave the keys as usual.

As we walked the short path from the car to the main building, I searched my surroundings. It was instinct. I knew Rafe was doing the same thing because instead of draping herself all over him, Diana was walking straight, her eyes shifting around as well.

I always found it interesting that she'd come after Rafe. And she'd managed to get past his defenses. Which, given who the hell Rafe was, was an anomaly. Of all the men whom I'd worked with since joining ORUS, Rafe was the outlier. He was like some kind of legend in the organization. But still, the beautiful blond with the killer eyes managed to slip past his lifetime of trusting no one.

A woman could do that to you.

Could that happen to me?

I had to figure out what the hell I was going to do about Gemma and about almost sleeping with her. And I still hadn't told Noah or Rafe about my suspicions concerning the Family. Like everything else, I needed to process that and come to my own conclusion before I brought it to Noah's attention. *Liar.*

Yes, there was a part of me that didn't want to add one last thing to the pile of shit. But that was because I was trying to keep everyone safe.

As expected, the moment they hit the penthouse, Rafe and Diana were giggling and pretty much running down to their room. Considering everything that had happened with the break-in, Noah had them all on premises again for safety. Hell, Rafe could barely wait. He just picked Diana up and tossed her over his shoulder caveman style. I shoved down the pang of envy.

As I scrubbed a hand through my hair, I headed down the hall and made a left toward my room. The moment I crossed the threshold I stopped short.

Gemma stood up from my bed. "I didn't think you were coming back."

"What the fuck are you doing here?"

She held up her hands as if to say she came in peace. "Dylan, he um, let me out yesterday. And also he let me back in. It's a long story. Nice guy."

"Why are you in my room?"

She stood stiff, openly staring at me. "I was shocked when I saw the stuffed toy. It brought back—all those memories." She was shaking on her feet and was playing with her fingernails. "I just—it's been so long. I thought they killed you. That's what Colin said he was going to do when they tossed me over the bridge... and I thought you were dead... or worse."

I stared at her. I knew if I took a step, even one step closer, I'd be sucked into her orbit, and I'd be trying out all those awesome skills I'd just learned. "I don't believe you."

She put a hand over her heart. "It's me, Gigi. I carried that Tigger around with me everywhere. You used to insist that I needed to learn to keep it clean or else I was going to get sick. And then you'd take it from me in the mornings sometimes and wash it, so that it would be. I remember that."

My heart squeezed. I *had* done that. But there was no way, no how, that this could be her.

But what if it is her?

I knew better. In my line of work, *what ifs* could get you killed, but I still couldn't help myself. I had to ask. "Where have you been?"

She inhaled deeply. "Being tossed over that bridge was the worst and best thing that's ever happened to me. I thought I was going to die. I couldn't swim, and I thrashed around in the water. The water was cold and tasted funny. I couldn't navigate how to swim or get to the bank or anything like that. I was so scared. It was black and... I don't know. I think a part of me just gave up. I was pretty sure I was dead."

I swallowed hard. "So where were you?"

"All I remember is being pulled out of the water. There was this woman— She was one of those women who look like they walk along the river during lunch: Chic. Beautiful. She was working near there or something. She called a nearby jogger to help pull me out of the water."

I frowned, trying to ascertain the truth of her statements. Was she lying? If she was, she was too good of a liar.

"I had no family. And I pretty much refused to go to the police. I freaked out when they even suggested that they'd send me to a hospital. I knew how the Family operated. I knew I'd end up right back in their hands. So I told them I would run if they called the police. The woman, she was a sort of social worker or something. She called a friend with child protection. They got me a place to stay for the night, but to make a long story short, she took me in. She eventually adopted me. She and her husband, they were really lovely. Eventually, she returned to where she was from, New York. My adoptive father passed away. She remarried, and the guy is a real prick." She vaguely gestured to her face. "That's my sad sack of a story. What about you? Where have you been? I tried to find you after I was brought to America. I— was told you were dead."

My gut knotted. There was a part of me that wanted to believe her story. There was something so sincere in her voice. I wanted to trust it. *But you know better.* "I never stopped mourning you. *Ever.* I would have come looking for you. You know that. But I couldn't. A few days after they tossed you over that bridge, they sold me. I never saw any of them again."

16

─────

Gemma

My heart skipped a beat.

They sold me.

When I was finally able to breathe again, I pressed a hand over my heart as if checking the organ was still intact. They'd sold him? I closed my eyes, caught between keeping my composure and mourning the sweet, protective boy he'd once been. I still remembered what he'd told Colin. That he intended to sell me himself. Deep down, I'd known it was a lie. I'd known he was trying to protect me at the time.

But maybe he'd just chosen to protect himself. All these years, I'd missed him but also carried such anger.

He'd promised to protect me and then just disappeared. I'd thought he'd escaped and run without looking back.

Instead he'd suffered a fate almost worse than death.

"Sold you to who?" I clamped my lips shut when my voice cracked. This wasn't the time to succumb to emotion. Not when there was so much to do and so little time.

I looked away. My question hung in the air unanswered but I didn't ask again. Although I knew where his story ended—he had been an ORUS agent after all—I wasn't sure I could handle hearing his journey to get there. Knowing the sick, twisted wankers who'd been chasing us that night, they'd probably sold him off to one of the ponces who liked young boys. To teach him a lesson.

To break him.

"Look, it's been a long night. Maybe we should get you settled in your room."

I sighed but then glanced behind me. The little stuffed Tigger stared back at me accusingly. Could I really walk away and leave him like this when he was obviously upset? Plus it wasn't like I was in the best frame of mind either. It was a scary but thrilling thing to have him back, to know that all these years he'd been missing me, too.

"I really missed you, Matt."

My soft declaration seemed to break down the last of his defenses. Matthias grabbed me and pulled me close, burying his face in my hair. Stunned, I didn't know what to do, so I let him. After a few moments, I found myself softening, and all of the emotions I tried to hide came barreling back. Years' worth of tears and frustration were no match for the stoic façade I'd cultivated.

"I have replayed that day, over and over," I whispered. "I thought you were gone forever."

That seemed to bring Matthias out of his grief. "If I could've gotten to you, nothing would have stopped me. But you were gone. I saw you face down in the water, not moving. They made me watch the river carry you away. I knew you couldn't swim." He shook his head. "I haven't been the same since. I think I died with you that day."

I hugged him tighter. "Do you think this is fate? Or the universe or whatever?"

"Bugger if I know," Matthias muttered. "As far as I'm concerned the universe can kiss my arse. It took you from me once. But I'll never let you go again."

His head lowered, and I knew this was the moment when everything would change. There were so many reasons to run. He had no idea I was here on a mission. My loyalty in the present was at war with the emotions from the past.

But none of that mattered. All I could think of was

that this was Matt. *My Matt.* And all of the feelings I had for him as a young girl had morphed and changed into something very different. Now he was so much more than just a protector. He was a man who intrigued and aroused me. The fact that I'd loved him so much once upon a time only added another layer of explosiveness to the chemistry burning between us now.

"I don't want you to let me go. I've never wanted that." I knew the effect of my words. Sure enough, his eyes darkened, and the intensity there made my breath catch.

Was I really going to do this? I wanted him. I needed him. I would find a way to protect us both...and Sabine. I couldn't let him go.

Then his head lowered and our lips touched, and I thought, *I'm never letting him go.*

It was a fantasy come to life. His lips were soft yet firm, and as his mouth moved over mine, I was all sensation. Even my skin felt like it was on fire, competing with the firecrackers in my blood. Matthias was just as intense as always. His strong arms locked behind my back, holding me in place. It was a strange thrill knowing that he wouldn't let me go.

Since when was I into cavemen? But I couldn't deny that I'd happily let him take me back to his cave as long as his mouth didn't stop what it was doing to my neck.

"That feels so good, Matt," I whispered.

Suddenly he pulled back. "My name really is Matthias. Mum shortened it when we went to live with the Family. I never got to tell you that before. I always regretted it. Everyone went by aliases back then, but I always wished that I'd been able to tell you before..."

I understood what he wasn't saying. Back then telling someone your name was a huge act of trust. As a child, I wouldn't have understood the importance of keeping it a secret, so I didn't blame him for not telling me. But I was thankful that he was sharing it now.

"Before it was too late," I finished for him.

"Yeah," he breathed.

I tugged at the front of his shirt, and he immediately pulled it over his head.

"Damn," I whispered appreciatively, noticing his dick twitching at my words. He liked that.

Matthias gripped his cock and squeezed. Then his eyes flew open and widened when my fingers covered his.

"Let me," I murmured right before I began to stroke him through the fabric of his jeans. Then I unzipped him and reached inside his boxers. When my eyes saw what was waiting for me, I paused. "Holy shit."

I glanced up at him, but his face was closed off. Did he think that I would be turned off? I reached down and gripped him firmly before sliding the tip of my finger gently over the Prince Albert piercing in the head of his cock.

"Well this is a surprise." I rubbed the pre-cum that was steadily leaking from the tip. "I wonder what that's going to feel like." Then I hooked my hands in the sides of his jeans and boxers and gently tugged them down.

"You don't mind?" he whispered, seeming almost afraid to hear the answer.

"No. I mean, it's not like I know anything about this stuff, but I've heard piercings feel good."

"You don't know anything about this stuff?" Matthias repeated.

I shook my head, sure my face was red. "I've never done this before. I mean, I've fooled around and stuff, but I don't really know what I'm doing."

Matthias nuzzled me, the gentle caress calming my fears.

"It's okay. I don't know either. That's why... what happened last night...happened. I haven't... done this before."

That was a shock, but I had a feeling that if I showed any surprise, he'd run out of there the same way he had last night. So I just resumed tugging at his jeans.

He stepped away to help me and shoved them down

along with his boxers. I stared at him in his full glory. Sweet baby Jesus at Tea Time, he was huge and gorgeous and...huge.

He backed me up to the bed and I scooted back to accommodate him. He pushed up on his arms to help me and then kicked them off and over the side of the bed.

"You really haven't done this before?" I finally asked. When he nodded, I grinned. "That makes me feel better then. I thought you ran off because I wasn't doing something right."

"You're right just by breathing," Matthias growled. Then he groaned as my hand tightened around his cock. "Although if you keep doing that, we'll have a repeat of last night and then where will we be?"

"Hmm, let's find out, shall we?" I slid a hand into his hair and then pulled him down for a kiss. As soon as our lips met, my hand started moving again and Matthias moaned helplessly into my mouth.

He was huge in my hand, and I could only hope I was doing it right. I'd only given one hand job before, and it hadn't been like this. Everything with Matthias was more intense, and I loved it.

I loved *him*. Always.

At the thought, my hand clenched around him and

he exploded, his hips pumping desperately as he moaned again and again.

He kept his eyes closed for a long time, like he didn't want to meet my gaze. But when he finally did, I raised my fingers to my mouth and licked delicately. His taste was slightly salty and made me crave the thought of him in my mouth. Matthias let out a strangled sound as he watched me lick my fingers.

And he was back. Instant hard-on.

"Would you look at that?" I smiled devilishly. "Not a bad start at all."

"I am so damn glad you're alive," Matthias blurted. "Sorry, that's a bit of a mood killer."

I just smiled and rested my head against his chest.

"It's okay. I'm pretty damn glad you're alive too. And that we found each other again."

"Yes. Yes we did." He scrambled off the bed and then bent down and picked me up, the sudden movement taking me off guard.

"Whoa. Where are we going?" I wrapped my arms around his neck. Not that I was worried he would drop me. I let my eyes roam over the defined muscles in his arms and chest. My childhood friend had turned into a well-built man.

"First, to the bathroom so I can put some cream on

these bruises. Then back to bed." His dark eyes fixed on mine. "Where you belong."

I gulped. A sharp stab of longing raced through me, shocking my nipples into sharp points and inducing a tight throb between my legs. It was overwhelming to be the focus of his complete attention, but this was what I'd been hoping for when I came here, right?

Now the only question was could I handle what I'd come for?

———

Matthias

I WAS in way over my head. But I'd also never felt more sure.

My heart was a drumbeat in my ears as I carried Gemma to the bathroom. She'd been stiff at first but slowly relaxed into my hold. When she rested her head against my neck and emitted a soft, relieved sigh, I'd almost come again. What the hell was it about this girl? Yes, we'd been special to each other years ago, but she had a hold on me unlike any other. Just the thought of her not being taken care of or not having something she needed sent my protective instincts into the red zone.

There was a driving beat inside me insisting that I take care of her. Protect her.

Pleasure her.

My face flamed at the thought, especially since I still had the smell of the sex club all over me. Somehow it seemed utterly wrong to have any part of that place touching Gemma. Rafe had been right. It wasn't what I thought it would be, but I wanted this to only be about us. I wanted her to have only the very best. The last thing she needed right now was some inept guy slobbering all over her.

It didn't keep my lips from connecting with her forehead as I set her down carefully on the counter in the bathroom.

The bruising on her face looked even worse under the harsh fluorescent lighting, but she was still absolutely perfect.

"You always were the most beautiful girl I'd ever seen."

Her eyes crinkled as she smiled. "You used to tell me that all the time. Total rubbish but it made me feel like a princess."

I pulled a tube of arnica from beneath the cabinet and then uncapped it. "It was nothing but truth."

She flinched when I placed my finger on her cheek. Then she leaned back slightly and pulled the shirt she was wearing over her head, leaving her in nothing but a plain black, cotton bra.

"It's ok. Go ahead," she said. I glanced up to find her watching me, her eyes following my every action greedily.

Fuck. She really was trying to kill me.

I paused then stroked the cream gently over the bruise that was currently somewhere between green and yellow. Rage flirted with the edge of my consciousness, and it was a true feat of strength that I ignored it. Ever since I'd seen the bruises on her face and then the others dotted over her ribs and thighs, I'd wanted to find her bastard of a stepfather and kick his ass.

"They don't hurt anymore," she stated, clearly tuning in to my distress. She'd always been able to do that, calm me down when I was on the verge of losing it.

"You should never have to be hurt. Ever. I'd like to find the bastard who did this to you and show him what's for."

Her lips quirked at that, almost as if she was amused. But then her arms wound around my neck and I stopped thinking.

"Why did you run last night?"

I stilled. "Blimey, Gemma. I came on your leg before we could even get things started."

Her eyes rounded. "Is that why you left? That didn't bother me at all."

She bit her lip, and the sight of her rolling the plump flesh between her teeth had my cock going ramrod straight.

"I actually thought that was pretty hot. Like you were so into me that you lost all control," she finished, peeking up at me through the wild waves of hair flopping over her forehead.

I barely heard her words before my lips were on hers again. This time she clearly wasn't content to be passive though because Gemma wrapped her legs around my waist, gripping me so tightly that I couldn't have escaped if I'd wanted.

But escape was the last thing on my mind. No, I was drunk on the way she looked at me and drowning in the soft sounds she made and the gentle caresses of her fingers in my hair.

I turned, my hands automatically going under her bottom to hold her steady. I could barely tell where I was going; it was pure muscle memory that got me from the bathroom back to my bed. But as soon as her back hit the mattress, Gemma let out another one of those arousing moans that almost made me come.

But I wasn't going to do that. This time, I was going to make sure we were both satisfied.

"You're so soft, Gemma. Everywhere." I was honored to touch the skin above her bra, the smooth skin tempting my fingers. She smelled warm, like something fresh-baked, and my mouth watered. No artificial fragrances for Gemma, just clean skin and woman.

I had never been more aroused in my life.

"I love the way you touch me." Gemma's mouth fell open as my lips followed my fingers.

I struggled for a few seconds but finally got her bra unhooked, and her small breasts were revealed. I lost my breath looking at the perky little nipples just begging for my mouth. I'd never forget the helpless, needy sound she made when I latched on. Her hands lodged in my hair, and her hips moved restlessly underneath me as she rubbed her core right against my stomach.

"Matthias!" Her eyes were languorous as she watched me dot kisses over her breasts and belly. I was sure this was all moving too fast, but nothing could stop this freight train now. Everything about Gemma was calling to me, enticing me. I needed to be inside her, to plant a mark and claim her.

In a flurry of movement, I stripped her of her remaining clothes, and we laughed breathlessly as we got tangled in the sheets. I kissed her until she was gasping, so overcome with happiness that I was sharing this first, awkward but magical moment with her. For the first time, I wasn't shamed or nervous. With Gemma, it was okay not to know everything because she'd always accepted me just the way I was.

Whatever we didn't know, we'd discover together.

I lost myself in the warmth of her skin, glorying over her softness and drowning in the combined fragrance of our arousal. By the time I fumbled into the night stand for a box of condoms Oskar had given me as a gag gift last Christmas, Gemma was covered in a light sheen of sweat and her eyes were squeezed closed.

"Are you sure?" I whispered.

When her eyes opened, the gentleness speared me straight to the core.

"Yes, Matthias. I've never wanted anything more in my life."

My hands were trembling as I ripped open the condom and rolled it on carefully. Gemma put a soft hand on my cheek, and when I looked up at her, she smiled.

"I'm so glad it's you."

A smile broke free then as I understood what she was really saying. This was her first time too, and she was happy to share it with me. Her hand tugged me down for a kiss and I settled right between her thighs.

When her arms wrapped around my neck, I pushed forward and then paused at her hiss of breath.

"Am I hurting you?" I whispered urgently.

Instantly her arms locked around my neck, holding me in place. "Don't you dare stop!"

I couldn't have even if I'd wanted to. She was so warm and tight, and the wet heaven I was sinking into was quickly stealing my ability for higher reasoning.

"Matthias... It feels so good," Gemma moaned against my lips, rocking her hips slightly to take me deeper.

I was lost. The sensations were too strong, and knowing that it was my Gigi there with me took me to a place where all of my defenses were down. We weren't vulnerable children anymore. I was a man now who could protect her. She was my family, and I had the tools now to defend what was mine. I growled and thrust deeper, my fingers clenching into fists as I was completely enveloped in her warmth.

Gemma let out a soft cry, and then her muscles went crazy, squeezing around me. The sight of her losing it was too much for me. Fuck, it felt good, the soft tugs on my cock combined with her warm, wet mouth tugging at mine. I could feel it coming, a tsunami of sensation, building up from the soles of my feet straight up my spine. I groaned as I came again, burying myself deep.

My arms tightened around her, clutching her close as we rode out the last pulses of our climax together. And the only thought I could hold on to was *I'm not letting go this time.*

Matthias

Waking up with a warm, curvy bottom against my stomach was on the list of things I had never thought would happen. My eyes opened, and I blinked at the sight of dark hair strewn across my pillow.

Gemma slept even wilder than I did.

I sat up slightly, careful not to wake her. She was sleeping on her side, facing away from me, and the sheets were all tangled around her legs. No wonder I'd woken up. I was freezing. I pulled the blanket she'd kicked off up higher and over my body.

It was crazy, but I couldn't stop smiling. If any of the guys saw me right now they'd give me shit for the rest of my natural life. But this kind of thing was no big deal for them. They'd probably woken up with women in their beds plenty of times.

Me, well, I'd always been on my own. After all the sick shit I'd been exposed to growing up, it was just easier to avoid all emotional entanglement, and I'd never really trusted anyone enough to go to sleep in their presence anyway.

And I hadn't missed it, or at least I hadn't *thought* I was missing anything. I'd structured my life to my specifications and I had been... satisfied. But being happy was an entirely new experience. I wasn't sure how to process this intensity of emotion.

Just then Gemma moaned softly and then rolled over, bumping into my chest. Her eyes flew open and she blinked at me in confusion. Then her eyes lit up and she grinned with such unabashed joy that I instantly knew I was done for.

Game Over. It's a wrap, I thought. *What man could resist a woman who made him feel like he was her favorite thing in the world?*

Had anyone ever been that happy to see me? It was overwhelming that seeing me could make her smile like that. But that was how Gemma made me feel. Like I was enough.

Like I was everything.

"Good morning," she murmured, turning her face into the pillow. "I'm sure I have morning breath."

"I don't care about that," I growled.

She shook her head frantically. "Yes you do. It's so gross!"

I laughed and then leaned down and tickled her playfully until she stopped hiding her face. Then I kissed her until she was moaning into my mouth and clutching my neck.

Because I could, damn it.

"This morning I want to get you into a safe house. We have one that's almost ready but I want to tweak a few things and make sure you're secure. Your stepfather will have no idea where you are."

For a moment her expression darkened, and I hated that I'd had to bring it up and take the smile from her face. But it was important that she know how to keep herself safe. If I couldn't be with her every moment, I was going to make sure she had the best security system money could buy.

"You don't need to do all of that. I'm sure I'll be okay."

I was already shaking my head. "Not enough. I can't take any chances with you."

I didn't say anything else, but she seemed to get it. Gemma sat up and kissed me softly on the cheek.

"Okay. When can we go see it?"

I climbed out of bed, thrilled at the blush that hit her cheeks when she realized I was completely nude. "After breakfast. That'll give me time to make sure everything is up and running and for the guys to do one last sweep of the neighborhood."

Gemma looked a little worried and she didn't lose the slightly stressed-out expression as we ate a quick but tasty breakfast of scrambled eggs and sausage. By the time we were in one of the company-issued black Jeeps, she still had a line in the middle of her forehead.

When we pulled up to the nondescript apartment building right on the edge of the East Village, I grabbed her hand.

"It's all going to be fine, yeah?"

She gave me a smile, but it didn't quite reach her eyes. "Thank you for this. I don't want you to think I'm ungrateful. I just feel bad that you and the other guys are doing all this work to hide me. I'm sure there are a lot of other people who need your help."

"You need our help."

She shrugged. "You know what I mean. People who *really* need it."

I couldn't understand why she would feel that way. She'd been hurt. I'd seen how vicious her bruises were with my own eyes. It still made me crazy that she wouldn't tell me her stepfather's name. I'd searched her identity online but couldn't find connections to either her mother or a stepfather. Otherwise I would have already paid the asshole a visit.

We took the stairs up to the third floor, and I scrutinized every aspect of the building, even though Rafe had personally recommended the location. The stairwells were wide and well-lit, and the hallways were clean. When we reached her unit number, I pulled the key from my pocket. We entered into a bright living room with honey-toned wood floors and an abundance of natural light.

"Oh Matthias. This is beautiful."

"Yeah it is. Rafe really found a gem." I didn't mention that we were probably only getting this place at a decent price because the owner of the building owed Rafe a favor or something.

"I can't believe this is all for me. It's huge!" Gemma walked further into the unit, exploring the kitchen.

I could hear her exclaiming over the new appliances as I checked out the security panel, adjusting a few of the settings and then making sure the changes registered in my central command program.

The longer we were there, the more agitated I started to feel. Usually at this point I was comfortable with the security, but for Gemma it just wasn't enough.

Let's face it, you won't think it's enough until she has a team of armed guards and basically lives in a Kevlar bubble.

I ran a hand over my face. I didn't want Gemma in this fucking apartment alone. I wanted her with me. Always. But it was way too soon to propose anything like that. Not to mention that it wasn't safe. I'd always lived my life like death was imminent. Taking revenge and laying out my plans, knowing that one day my number would be up. I'd been fine with that when it was just me, but I didn't want my karma landing on Gemma. Ever. My Tigger didn't deserve that. Her life had been hard enough, and just like when we were kids, all I wanted to do was protect her.

A sudden knock on the door startled us both. My hand went to the gun in my waistband before I realized the security panel was already streaming an image of our visitor.

Gemma peered over my shoulder. "Oh it's Rafe and Oskar!" She unlocked the door and pulled it open before I could respond.

I gritted my teeth. We were going to have a little conversation about opening the door before fully assessing the situation. What if there had been someone lurking in the hallway behind my friends, waiting for a chance to strike when she opened the door?

Obviously anyone who tried that with me, Rafe and

Oskar around had a death wish, but it could happen when she was here alone and one of her friends came to visit. She had to be more careful. This was New York City, after all.

"Hi! Come on in. Thanks again for finding this place for me. It's amazing." Gemma ushered Rafe and Oskar in like old friends, and of course like the bastards that they were, they were just eating it up.

Especially Oskar, who kept shooting amused glances at me every time Gemma would smile at them or touch their arms. I gritted my teeth. The big blond bastard knew damned well how irritating it was to see my girl touching them so familiarly.

"We just wanted to come check on you. See how you like the place," Oskar drawled.

The bastard made it sound like he'd come out of his way just to check on her, I thought grumpily. It was standard procedure for them to check on a new client once they were put in a safe house. But of course Gemma didn't know that. By her smile, she thought Oskar and Rafe had made a special trip just for her. It took quite a bit of willpower to keep me from pointing out that they were just doing their jobs.

"I appreciate it so much. This is a great apartment." Gemma ushered them into the living room like they were guests coming over for tea.

Rafe, clearly reading the mounting rage on my face, walked toward the kitchen and away from the group. Oskar just grinned broadly and hovered next to Gemma. Right next to her. Then he put his arm around her shoulders casually. Oh hell no.

"Back the fuck up, asshole!" I barked, then immediately wished I hadn't when Gemma gasped.

She glanced between the two of us warily. "Is everything okay?"

Oskar removed his arm, way too slowly for my liking. I bared my teeth.

"Everything is fine. There are just a few things we need to check on, and then we'll leave you to it." Oskar gave me a knowing look before he walked toward the hallway leading to the bedrooms.

Gemma

I WATCHED as Oskar walked away. When I turned back around, Matthias was glaring at his back like the other man was a threat or something. He didn't lose the feral look until our eyes met and the careful, blank mask he usually wore dropped over his features like a shield.

There he is, I thought. It was amazing how he could

turn it off and on again at will. I was starting to understand why everyone referred to him with reverence. He was skilled at keeping himself concealed, revealing only what he wanted you to see. But I'd seen the real Matthias, the one forged on a cold afternoon when our hope had been built up and lost in the span of one afternoon.

"You didn't have to be so rude, you know? He was just being nice." I couldn't resist teasing him a bit. It should have rankled me that he was acting like a caveman. It wasn't like I was some delicate little flower.

But honestly, I'd gotten a little thrill when he'd growled at the other man like that. It was obvious that he didn't want any other man near me, which was archaic but still sexy as hell.

"He needs to do his fucking job," Matthias muttered before he turned back to the security panel.

I smothered my grin. He didn't seem to know how to handle his jealousy either, which made sense if he hadn't had many girlfriends. Or any, I thought, remembering his confession that I was his first. It seemed so hard to believe.

The thought reminded me of the type of life he'd led, the places he'd been. It brought a damper on things to know that he'd kept to himself because of all the shit the Family had put him through. He was likely the only person who'd really understand why I was doing this.

I turned away and squeezed my hands together. It was so tempting to confide in him. To tell him everything and let him protect me the way he done so many times in the past.

Stick to the plan.

Even though I doubted I'd spend much time here, I walked up behind him and peered at the security panel. It looked pretty standard, but knowing Matthias he'd added some modifications or something. He wasn't an out-of-the-box kind of guy. If he was going to believe that I was the damsel in distress, I needed to play the part.

"Would you mind walking me through this security system?" I smiled at him. It seemed to put him at ease because his shoulders dropped and he lost the tight, pinched look around his eyes.

Matthias started pointing things out, but I was only half paying attention. Now that I'd opened that line of thought, it was all I could think about, telling Matthias and getting his help. He would likely be able to come up with some high tech way to get Sabine out, maybe hack his way into the Family and find out when their defenses would be lowest. They could plan a coordinated attack, get Sabine, and free as many of the women still enslaved there as possible.

It would be risky no matter how I sliced it. This whole thing was one breath away from disaster, and I was hyper-aware that it was my friend's life on the line if anything didn't go according to plan. *That's why you should tell Matthias*, my mind suggested helpfully. *He can help you. When has he ever let you down?*

But even as I thought it, my mind produced a much more likely scenario; *me* letting *him* down. Matthias putting his life on the line for me. Again.

Getting hurt. Again.

He'd already been down that road once and had to watch me almost drown in the icy water of the Thames. Everything he'd gone through had been because he'd tried to get me to safety.

I wouldn't do that to him again. This time I was going to save him.

Whether he'd welcome it or not.

"Hey, are you okay?" Matthias had finally clued in to my mood and was watching me with narrowed eyes.

I fixed a smile on my face. "No, everything is fine. It's just a lot to remember."

He didn't look convinced, but he didn't push, for which I was grateful. It was going to be hard enough to keep this from him. I didn't think I would have the willpower to lie to him while he was being so sweet.

I bit my lip. If I couldn't resist him already, what the hell was I going to do when it was time to hand him over to ORUS?

18

———————

Matthias

The next day, I watched Gemma carefully. Something was wrong. It didn't matter how much time had passed between us—I knew her, inside and out.

Now you know her body too.

Despite myself, my heart rate ticked up just remembering her taste, and that breathy little sound she made just before she came. *Yeah, this is not helping.* She didn't need the part of me that couldn't get enough of her. She needed the part of me that had loved her since we were kids. "You want to tell me what's wrong?"

She looked up from the book she'd been reading. "Nothing. I'm fine. Good. I promise."

I chuckled low. "Yeah, I don't believe you. You're forgetting, love: I know you."

A blush crept up her neck. "It's nothing you need to worry about. I swear. I'm happy that I have you now. I promise. You can stop worrying."

Stop worrying? For ten years I thought she was dead. Gone. I thought I'd been unable to protect her. And now she was back and she thought I could just let it go? Not bloody likely.

"When are you going to get it? I can feel that something is off with you. It's like that first time that we met. Do you remember? You were so little. The other kids, they thought that survival was a solitary game and didn't want to help you. But I knew how much you needed me. I couldn't leave you to your own devices then."

She gave me a soft, wistful smile. "You walked right up to me and said, 'I'm Matt. I'm going to take care of you now.'"

My lips tipped up into a smirk. "I could barely take care of myself. I had no business trying to take care of you too."

She smiled at me. "Are you kidding? Without you I would have died within a week."

I shook my head. "You were tougher than you gave yourself credit for. I mean, hell, look at you now. After everything you've been through, you're still so incredibly strong."

I joined her on the bed and tugged her to me, laying her head on my shoulder. "Whatever is going on, whatever you're afraid of, just let me know. I will slay those dragons or die trying. Right now, it seems even death can't keep us apart. I love you, Gigi. I'm starting to think the reason I haven't had a heart all this time is because it's been with you."

She pulled back. Her gaze searched mine. "I have never forgotten you. There have been a million times when I pretended that you survived that place and you were happy somewhere. That maybe, just maybe, you'd made it to your gran's house." She frowned. "I guess neither of us ever made it."

I shook my head. "No, we didn't. But we made it somewhere better; back to each other."

Her smile was tremulous. And then she launched herself into my arms. For a second, my mind went through all the variations of how to respond. And then I just went with the one that felt the best—locking my arms around her and holding her tight.

I pulled her onto my lap and cradled her against me. That move shouldn't have resulted in her somewhat straddling me as she tucked her head into the crook of my neck, but it did. When she pulled back, I stared into the eyes of the girl I'd never been able to forget. And finally, my brain was able to make the connection between the girl who once needed me and the woman she was now. I vowed right then to myself that I would protect the both of them with my life. The two versions of her became my everything.

I slid my hands into the hair at her nape and fisted, angling her head and kissing her deep.

I kissed her with the passion of a starving man. I kissed her with all the love I didn't know how to express. I kissed her with the worry I'd had for her over the years. I kissed her with the grief that I'd felt when I thought she was dead. I kissed her with the lust coursing through my veins.

I poured everything I had into that kiss. Thanks to her, I knew what the hell love was. I saw what the big fucking deal was. That driving, desperate, and urgent need to be with your partner? I finally got it. This could be my life. And I wanted it. When she was this close, that monster inside me didn't exist anymore.

———

Gemma

TELL HIM THE TRUTH.

It would be so simple to just tell him the damn truth, to open my mouth and have the words spill out, and then he would know everything.

My Matt. My Matthias. But would that put him in danger? Would just being with him put him in danger? I was walking a fine line between endangering him and saving him. Right now, everyone wanted a piece of him. And I needed to make some decisions. If I wasn't careful, I would get myself, him, *and* Sabine killed, and Father would continue terrorizing people.

Matthias fisted his hands in my hair again and I moaned, rocking my hips over him. Why was this so good? Was it supposed to be this good? It was like the two of us just fit together in a way that made me feel that my skin was on fire, like my hair was in flames.

As he kissed me deeper, the thick length of him twitched inside his boxers. I could feel every inch of him against my core. And God help me, I wanted him again... *needed* him again. Would this feeling ever stop? Would there ever come a time when I didn't need to touch him?

That time is probably coming sooner than you know. You can't sustain this. And when he finds out, either he's going to kill you or leave.

I shoved the thought aside. I knew now that he would never hurt me. He would be angry, yes. Was it possible he would never forgive me? Absolutely. But hurt me? No. Not Matt. Despite what he thought about himself, I knew better. He was not capable of it. He licked into my mouth again, demanding that I focus on him and on the way he was making me feel, and I was more than happy to oblige.

"Matthias," I whispered on a moan.

Our movements were frenzied and quick as we devoured each other. With a frustrated groan, he yanked the T-shirt I'd been wearing over my head. Then he ducked and suckled my breasts as he whispered homage to them. While he licked and teased with his tongue and teeth, he tormented and pinched my other nipple gently, sending shockwaves of desire ricocheting through me.

I dug my nails into his back as I rotated my hips, meeting each shallow thrust with one of my own. I felt the tingling at the base of my spine, and I tugged on his hair. "Matthias."

I could feel his smile against my neck and knew what was coming. "I was wondering if I could make you come just from this."

I knew he preferred to watch me. Matthias gripped

my hips, his fingers digging in as they ground against each other. Shit. I wasn't going to be able to hold this. I moaned low, throwing my head back.

He slid a hand to where our bodies met and stroked his thumb over my clit through my panties. The teasing sensation on the bundle of nerves sent me crashing over the edge. My pussy convulsed, begging for his hard length.

Matthias

I STARED up at the woman on top of me, her skin practically glowing in the dim light of the room. With every glance from under her lashes, and every tentative touch of her fingertips, my whole body felt like it was on fire, being stoked to full blaze.

Vaguely, I wondered if spontaneous combustion was a myth. Add in the euphoric feeling that surged through my blood every time she touched me, and I was likely to come in my boxers.

With every pant as she came down from ecstasy, her rose-tipped breasts swayed as she shifted her straddle further down my legs. Her hands came into contact with the elastic of my boxers, and my cock throbbed and strained. Involuntarily, my hips rose, and I tried to school my breathing.

Lying back on the bed, trying to get my shit under control, I arched my back. I snatched a pillow off the bed, shoving it over my face to muffle the cry.

Her hands paused. "Should I stop?"

"Jesus, God, please don't." I might consider crying if she did. It didn't matter how many times she touched me, each time felt like the first.

Slim-fingered, delicate hands tugged my boxers down and I lay before her, naked as the day I was born.

Her eyes traveled from my toes up my shins, up to my thighs, and fixated on my cock.

Unable to not respond to the look of lust written all over her face, my cock jerked, and her eyes went wide. She shimmied back up my body, straddling me again at the knees. She supported her hands on either side of me.

"Has anyone ever told you you're very big?"

I grinned. "Nope. You're the first."

She cocked an eyebrow, then resumed her inspection of my body. When she leaned directly over my straining cock, her long hair brushed against my skin, and her breath floated over my dick. It only took two puffs of breath from her, and my control snapped.

My hands banded around her biceps, and I hauled her up against me so I could kiss her. Flipping her over on her back, my hand fisted on the elastic of her very small panties, flexed, then ripped. I needed nothing between us.

I wedged a knee between her thighs. "Condoms. Shit, we might be out."

She blinked at me rapidly, her tongue peeking out to moisten her lips. "I'm on the pill. I—I've never…"

I shushed her with a gentle kiss to her sternum. "Shh. I just want to make you feel good. Will you let me?"

She trembled underneath me even as she nodded. Against my thigh, I could feel the moisture of her slick core. I tried not to think about how soft she would be. I needed to go slow. My cock, on the other hand, had a mind of its own and pulsed against her thigh.

I gave her another peck on the lips before tracing feather-light kisses along her jaw. When I nuzzled her neck, she giggled. When I went from nuzzling to nibbling, she moaned. My hands enjoyed free reign of her breasts, testing the weight of the full globes, teasing the tight buds to pucker. Her hips rose to meet me every time I tugged on one of the tips.

I placed open-mouthed kisses on her clavicle and her chest, eventually making my way to her breasts. But no matter how much she shifted, I didn't kiss her nipples. Not even when her hands tried to pull my head to her breasts. Though I wanted to taste them again, there was somewhere else I needed to be.

My lips continued a path down her ribs to her belly button. When the tip of my tongue dipped into the tiny crevice, she parted her thighs on an exhale.

Gemma dug her hands into my hair when I kissed my way to the top of her mound. I knew beneath the soft curls I'd find what I'd been waiting for.

Lifting my head, I watched her expression as I parted her slick folds with my thumb. She widened her legs and transferred her hands to dig at the sheets. Gently circling the nub of her clitoris with my thumb, I eased one finger into her slick, dewy channel. Immediately, her muscles clenched around my finger, and a tingle started at the base of my spine. Shit. All I was doing was touching her, and I was already so near coming. I tried breathing deep and focusing on her pleasure. I could wait.

Slowly, my finger retreated then entered her again. When she exhaled, she whispered my name. The soft "Matthias" filled the silence in the room. All I wanted was to hear her say it again. I slid my finger inside her again with an achingly slow retreat, and she whispered, "Oh, God."

When I slid two fingers in, she stilled, and I paused to give her a chance to get used to the motions. She didn't like my consideration. "Why are you stopping?"

"I don't want to hurt you."

"I want—" She frowned. "I don't know what I want, but I know I need you."

I bit back a curse as I kissed her thigh. "You're not ready yet."

With slow, precise motions, she rotated her hips under my hands, coating my fingers with her juices. "I'm ready. If you just—"

With her hips doing half the work, I began moving my fingers again, gently making love to her while my thumb stroked her pleasure button. Her hips began to move in time with increasing tempo. She rode my fingers, and I was mesmerized by the pink flesh of her core surrounding them. The surge of need nearly blinded me, and I hastily removed my fingers, ignoring the protest from her, and instead replaced them with my tongue.

Gemma gasped and sat up in the bed, but I didn't stop, just held her legs wide, splaying her softness to me. While my thumbs parted her folds, I lapped at the sensitive flesh as she quivered around my tongue. The more I lapped at her, the wetter she became. She tasted sweet and spicy like her scent suggested, and the combination was heady.

I could tell the moment she gave into the sensations. She lay back against the sheets and held my head in place while trying to widen her thighs. Tracing circles around her clit with my tongue, I drove her higher and higher, until her whole body tensed.

Her inner walls quivered against my questing tongue, and her breathing came out in labored puffs. Placing a gentle kiss on the sensitive skin of her clitoris, I drew myself back up her body, using my elbows as support. She blinked up at me with wide eyes.

"Wow."

"You sure do know how to stroke a guy's ego, don't you?" I drawled.

Gemma reached between us, and her delicate fingers closed around the rigid length of me. My vision blurred, and my balls started to tingle. I dropped my forehead to hers. "Jesus, Gemma, I want you so bad."

Her eyes fluttered closed, and she moaned. "I'm yours. Always yours." She pumped my cock with her palm, once, then twice. The trembling in my body started in my legs first. Maybe it was right what they said about guys and their erections—the blood drained from their feet first so they couldn't run away.

"Love, I—"

She pumped me again, but this time brought my cock to her dewy center. I hissed a breath and squeezed my eyes shut, praying I didn't come before I was inside her. Blinking rapidly, I gazed into her eyes. Gritting my teeth and inching forward into her tight sheath.

"Fuck, Gemma." I pushed in to the hilt, and she hissed beneath me. I tried not to move, to let her get accustomed to me and breathe for a minute. But that voice in my head wouldn't stop. *Rush. Take. Brand.* I knew from before that she'd been sore. I worried I'd been too eager so I was trying to take my time.

I withdrew by increments, and she hissed again. But this time when I surged forward, she moaned. I planted a kiss on her lips again and waited for her gaze to meet mine. "Are you sure you're okay?"

Her breathing still ragged, she slowly smiled up at me. "Yes. Matthias, please don't stop."

That was all the invitation I needed. Withdrawing to the tip of my cock, I surged forward, keeping up that slow and steady tempo until she started to claw at my back. Her hips pumped against mine, her velvet sheath swallowing the length of me.

I felt the walls of her slick lining start to convulse against me once more. Knew now what was coming. "Hold on to that feeling, baby. Ride it out. Enjoy the feeling." I kissed her deep, one hand tugging at the tip of her breast. The other reached between us, my thumb finding the dew-slick button and circling it.

Gemma threw her head back, arching her back and giving me unfettered access to her breast. "Matthias!" she called my name on a breath as her body shook beneath me.

As she rode the wave, I continued to drive into her. Longing to keep her ride going as long as I could. Wishing I could stay like this forever.

I muttered a curse as my balls began to ache. I needed to come, but I wanted her to come again for me. I wanted to feel her body melt into mine one more time. I kissed her again before withdrawing completely. My cock gave a jerk of protest.

With a growl, I shoved a hand under her back, grabbing onto her waist. Flipping her over onto her stomach, I glided a hand down her smooth back to her perfect, round ass. I drew her limp body up onto her knees. Leaning into her, I whispered, "Hold onto the headboard."

She flicked me a cocked eyebrow over her shoulder, but she complied.

"That's a good girl. Now spread your knees for me." When she parted her legs, I bit back a groan. That angle gave me the world's most perfect view of her ass. Shifting behind her, I covered her body with mine again. "Are you sore, love?" As I asked, I inserted one finger in her still slick pussy, and she moaned.

"A—a—little."

But that didn't stop her from moving her hips in time with my questing finger. When I added another finger, she sucked in a quick breath of air, but then moaned as my fingers retreated.

"Matthias, please. I just need—"

I lined my cock up with her sweet opening and whispered as I slid my cock into her pussy. "I know. I need you too."

There was no way I could last. This felt too good. As I held her hips tight and rode her, she called my name. Leaning over her as our hips locked, I played with her breasts, relishing their sweet response to my touch. Just by hovering over the sensitive skin of her nipples, they puckered in anticipation, inviting me to touch, to tease, to pinch.

She let her head land between her braced shoulders as she pushed her hips back to meet my every stroke. "God, that feels, so—"

I knew the instant she started to come again. Her pussy began to milk my cock, and her whole body shook. I could only hold on for the ride, digging both hands into the curves of her ass.

As she shattered around me, my vision started to

grey at the edges. The tingle that had started in my spine felt more like someone had hooked me up to thousand-volt electrodes as I pumped inside of her. So close to heaven.

As blinding light exploded my vision, my whole body erupted in electric bliss.

19

Matthias

I was warm again and was that... I grinned as my dick registered that, yes, there was a plump ass rubbing against it right then. As if on cue, adrenaline surged, and I was instantly hard as a rock.

Waking up with Gemma would never get old.

I clamped the covers down with my arm and cuddled her closer. It was hilarious to me that even though she slept wild as hell, her ass always seemed to find me in the night, like a homing beacon. There must be some signal my dick was sending out that drew her in.

And I was grateful for it, I thought as my hands

skimmed over the soft, generous curves within reach. Plus she smelled fucking amazing.

"Good morning, Tigger." My voice was always rough in the mornings but it sounded like I'd swallowed gravel.

Gemma moaned once and flopped over on her stomach. The position put the round globes of her ass on display since the T-shirt she'd slept in had ridden up around her waist. I reached out and caressed the smooth skin on her hip. She was so soft. Everywhere. She purred at my touch and wiggled her ass. Her hair flipped up, exposing the back of her neck. I climbed over her, ready to start the morning off right when I noticed the cluster of moles on the back of her neck. Then I lost my breath.

They weren't moles.

I climbed off her carefully, moving slowly so as not to wake her. But I didn't even need to get a second look at the pattern of black dots I'd seen on her skin. My memory was excellent and besides that, I'd recognize an ORUS tattoo anywhere. The dots on her neck were of the constellation *Persephone.*

Shaking, I stood next to the bed, my mind racing over the facts at hand. Thinking of something, I glanced back at the sleeping woman in my bed, noting the lack of dots on her wrists. A wave of relief rushed through me.

"This is crazy," I muttered. After all, I'd heard of Agent Persephone. She'd been one of the few new recruits trained from childhood because her mother was also an agent. I'd never met her, but I'd heard the stories.

Badass females weren't a rarity in ORUS but there was no denying the organization was male dominated. Female agents were generally known by all because they were so valuable. They were able to operate under the radar, gaining trust and access to places easily because people underestimated them. Especially in the types of places ORUS infiltrated, women were seen as toys or pawns. Never as a threat. Some of the organizations most dangerous missions had been led by female agents.

I'd know if one of them was sleeping next to me at night. Right?

Unable to shake the mounting panic, I stood. I had to think logically. If she was ORUS, she would be marked on the neck, wrists and the soles of her feet. Her wrists weren't marked, I could see that. I moved to the end of the bed where one of Gemma's bare feet stuck out from under the covers.

A pattern of black dots covered the soles of both feet.

"Fucking hell," I muttered as my heart rate accelerated so fast I almost passed out.

I snatched my clothes from the floor next to the bed,

almost straining my neck as I yanked the shirt over my head. There should have been a litany of ideas rolling through my mind but honestly everything was blank. Empty. That was how I felt.

Like the one thing I could count on to be real had just crumbled in my hand like dust.

I'd left my laptop up front in the living room. Careful not to make too much noise, I carried it to the kitchen counter. Even though I already knew what it meant, there was a part of me that needed to see it in black and white. And sure enough, a few minutes later I was looking at the classified ORUS file for Agent Persephone.

Also known as Gemma Boyd.

"Oh fuck me," I groaned and placed my forehead to the cold countertop. There were too many things going through my mind right now, and I wasn't even sure where to start. But after a few moments of chaos, I called on the icy reserve that had carried me through years of training and torture. Any emotions I'd experienced for the woman in my bed were now buried under the one thing I knew would never let me down.

Purpose.

I closed the laptop and stalked back to the bedroom. Gemma was still face down in the bed, half buried under the covers. I kicked the side of the mattress. She jumped up, her hands fisted and her eyes swinging around the room.

I shook my head. How had I missed it? She reacted like someone who'd been trained, not a civilian.

"What's going on?" She relaxed when she saw me standing next to the bed.

It was a struggle to ignore how beautiful she looked all mussed from sleep and the aftereffects of their lovemaking the night before. But she was no longer Gemma, my lover. Now she was the enemy. A spy sent to infiltrate the only home I'd ever had.

"We need to talk. Get dressed. You have five minutes."

Her eyes widened at my tone. "What's going on? What's happened?"

There was nothing to indicate that she was anything other than a scared woman on the run. How stupid had I been? She hadn't even had to work to get past my defenses. All she'd had to do was smile at me and I'd been done for. ORUS never let you go; it had been my worst fear and now it was here. Noah had promised that he'd get us out, and I hadn't believed it until we'd actually walked away without getting a bullet through each of our skulls. But I should have known the organization had just been biding its time before finding a way to strike back.

Had Ian known of their past together and decided to use it against him?

Gemma climbed to her knees on the bed, watching me warily. "Are you okay? Matthias, you're scaring me."

"Just get cleaned up." I watched her climb out of the bed hastily before snatching up her clothes from the floor. Her cheeks pinkened when she saw me watching her.

I turned and walked out of the room, fighting the conflicting feelings banging around my chest. She'd looked so hurt, and my first instinct was to comfort her, to assume there was some misunderstanding and she hadn't really been lying to me.

There's no way to misunderstand her pretending to need Blake Security's help. I grimaced. She'd come there pretending to be injured so we'd take her in. And I'd fallen for it.

In the kitchen my laptop was still open. It didn't take long to find what I needed. As soon as Noah had installed Ian as the new head of ORUS, I had figured they'd need a back door in to keep on top of what the shadow organization was up to. So I was able to navigate through Ian's private files quickly now that I knew what I was looking for.

Anything tied to Agent Persephone.

By the time Gemma walked up behind me, I had

read seventy five percent of her current mission file and was halfway through her training files.

I was also one hundred percent enraged.

———

Gemma

SLEEPING IN WAS BLISS. I knew I should get up, but having a bit of a lie in wasn't something I got to do often. Plus it wasn't like I was alone. Matthias was there. I could afford to relax a bit since he was there keeping an eye on things. It was an unfamiliar luxury, to be able to relax and know that someone else had my back.

I had never been the type to go dreamy-eyed over a guy. Not that there had been much time for that kind of thing anyway. Andromeda didn't play around when it came to training. So instead of sleepovers and giggling about boys, I had spent my preteen years in combat training and at target practice. By the time I'd been formally recruited into ORUS, I'd been almost as good a sniper as some of the men Andromeda worked with.

But when it came to things like this—I curled up and smiled to myself at the thought of getting naked with Matthias again—I was as green as a teenager for sure. It wasn't just the physical part, but it was the sense of safety. The anticipation of seeing him again. The excitement of being together and discovering who we'd be as a couple.

But you're lying to him.

The thought didn't sit well but it couldn't be ignored. I'd come on this mission with no idea who the target was. No one could have predicted the way things had panned out. Protecting Sabine had been my only priority, but things had changed now. Matthias was a priority too.

It was time to tell him the truth. All I could hope for was that he would let me explain.

Just then something hard hit the bed. Instinct had me on my knees with my fists up in the blink of an eye. Matthias stood next to the bed watching me with fire in his eyes.

And I knew my time was gone.

"What's going on?" I forced my hands down, trying to look relaxed. I didn't want to assume anything. There could be any number of reasons why he had murder in his eyes. Maybe he didn't know anything yet and was upset about something at work.

"We need to talk. Get dressed. You have five minutes." Matthias wouldn't meet my eyes.

Shit. He definitely knew something. "What's going on? What's happened?"

Mentally I started running through the scenarios. We'd fought once, and even though I was skilled at hand to hand, I couldn't beat him. I knew that. Plus I didn't want to fight him. It was bad enough that he was looking at me like something gross he'd stepped in, but if I had to physically defend myself, I thought my heart might crack right down the center.

"Are you okay? Matthias, you're scaring me. What's going on?"

"Just get cleaned up."

I climbed from the bed and grabbed my clothes off the floor. His eyes bored into my side as I moved; I could feel the heat of his hatred even from several feet away. When our eyes met, Matthias spun around and walked out of the room.

I let out a breath I hadn't realized I was holding. What the hell was I going to do? Worse, what was Matthias planning? I needed to find a way to contact Ian. Do some damage control. But first I needed to find out what Matthias knew. Had he discovered inconsistencies in my story? Maybe he was just upset that I'd lied about my background and where I'd come from. That wasn't so bad; I could spin that. Then once he'd calmed down some, I could figure out a way to break the truth.

After washing up quickly, I left the bedroom and walked down the hall to the kitchen. Matthias stood with his back to me, looking at something on his laptop. When I got closer, I saw it was a picture of me.

Fuck. It was my ORUS profile.

"That's classified," I whispered. What the hell was going on? I'd never known anyone to have access to agent profiles except for Orion himself.

Matthias clicked a button, and my profile increased in size. My own eyes stared out at me accusingly from the picture. Probably wondering what the hell I was still doing there. I might have known and loved Matthias as a child, but he'd been trained by the same ORUS I was trying to escape from. He wouldn't take this betrayal lightly, and I couldn't assume he'd give me mercy just because we were lovers.

Run. Get away from him while you still can.

But before I could move toward the door, Matthias spun around and locked one arm around my throat, spinning me until I was facing the other direction and couldn't move without crushing my neck under his forearm.

Years of training weren't for nothing though, and I wasn't going out without a fight. I thrust my elbow back, hearing him grunt in surprise and then dropped low as soon as the tension in his arm slackened. I kicked up, catching him in the thigh, and then rolled away before he could grab me. With the kitchen counter between us, we eyed each other distrustfully.

"What? Are we going to fight to the death now?" I shook my head sadly. "I can explain if you let me. You know I wasn't trying to hurt you. In your heart, I believe you know that."

Matthias closed his eyes, as if it was agony to even look at me. "You're ORUS, so all I know is I can't trust anything you say."

"So what do we do? Fight? I'm still healing from the last time."

His eyes rounded. "Bloody hell. That was you. Of course it was."

I hated the disgust in his voice. He had just started to open up to me and now we were all the way back to square one. If that.

"I was sent on a mission, it's true, but I had no idea you were the target."

"Bullshit," Matthias spat. "ORUS is nothing if not thorough. They wouldn't send an agent after me without giving them every detail, from what training I've had to whether I take a shit in the morning or the afternoon."

I debated whether I should tell him that the mission hadn't been from ORUS. I hadn't been cleared by Orion to discuss it with anyone, and it could compromise everything if Matthias discovered the Family was after him and decided to retaliate. Would they take their anger out on Sabine?

"I want to tell you everything, but I can't. Please understand," I pleaded. "It's not my life on the line here."

Matthias leapt over the counter and snagged my wrist. "Yes it is. You just haven't realized it yet."

He pulled something from his pocket and wrapped it around my wrist. When he finally let me go, I saw that he'd clamped a tracker on my wrist.

"Where are you taking me?" I asked finally. Now that he had me tagged, there was no point in running. I wouldn't be able to hide from him even if I could make it out the door.

"To the penthouse. You took all the trouble of breaking in there, now you're going to explain to the team exactly why."

20

Gemma

I WAS LOCKED in Noah's office with three killers. As scenarios went, I'd had better. But I'd gotten myself into this mess and I could get myself out. My one saving grace was that there were glass walls. So, it was unlikely they would murder me with their wives and babies walking around.

Noah, Rafe, and Matthias just glared at me. Okay, make that Noah and Rafe glared. Matthias stayed close to me as if ready to restrain me if I tried to run or leave. Rafe and Noah sat on the other side of the table.

I understood what was happening here. There was

no escape, and they were going to get answers. The easy way or the hard way.

Noah turned his gaze on me. "Start talking. And it had better be the truth, because if it's not, I'll let Matthias kill you."

I dared a glance at Matthias. I wasn't sure exactly what they thought, but I knew for sure he wasn't going to kill me. That's not who he was, at least not with me.

I tipped my chin up. "I'll tell you the truth."

Noah just glared at me. Rafe? He scoffed. Matthias sat silent and unmoving. "Okay, you obviously understand the situation. I work for Ian. I've been an ORUS agent for some time."

Rafe shook his head. "Specificity is your friend right now." I drew in a shuddering breath. His voice was flat, cold, deadly. It gave me goose bumps.

"Fair enough. I was rescued from my fall into the river at age eight. My adoptive mother's name was Adaline. Andromeda is her code name. She was also an ORUS agent. She brought me back to the States and treated me as her own. I was raised mostly by her partner. Given all those normal kid things. When I turned fourteen, she started training me. The previous Orion allowed her to personally manage most of my training. When I graduated a year ago, I became a full-time agent. My current assignment is undercover with the Family. I didn't know that Matthias was the target. Once I knew who he was, it complicated things. Ian was aware, and he wanted me to secure Matthias's safety."

Noah's brows shot up. "So Ian knows you're here?"

"Well, unless he's found another way to track me besides my phone, then he doesn't know my exact location. But he knows I'm undercover with you and that I'm trying to bring Matthias out safely."

Matthias still hadn't said a thing. Hadn't responded to me. Hadn't even looked at me. He was just staring straight ahead, very likely over Rafe's shoulder.

Rafe sat back in his seat. "So we're supposed to believe that Ian sent you here to save Matthias?"

"Yes, but it's more complicated than that. They put me undercover with the Family because I had knowledge of them from when I was a child. I knew the ins and outs. I could identify the players, who was important and who wasn't. And I was under for about three months. Father was my ultimate target. But while inside, I found my old childhood friend, Sabine. She's been there all along, and they have her working as a drug mule. It's a terrible situation. They've been testing my loyalty. When I refused to blindly kill, they took Sabine."

So far, Noah and Rafe hadn't said anything, so I continued.

"I've been passing other tests. They gave me one last test which was to come here and to neutralize the target. After that, I would get the opportunity to meet Father. I was given a name and an address, and so I tried to execute on that. You all know how that turned out."

Rafe frowned. "You were the one who broke in?"

I nodded. "I wasn't after the baby. I was after him." I glanced at Matthias again. "You saw that fight. I never meant for any of this to happen. When I realized how well-trained he was, I called it in to Ian to try and find out what the hell was going on. It wasn't until then that he knew who the target was."

Noah crossed his arms. "Oh don't you worry. I'll be dealing with Ian."

I believed him too. His mouth was set in a firm line. The muscle of his jaw ticked with every movement of his lips, as if anger coursed through his blood. I'd really made a mess of things. The problem was, now that he knew who I was, there was no going back. No going back to that innocent moment when it was just Matt and Gigi again.

"Ian wanted Matthias safe. Obviously, I couldn't carry out the hit. He's good. He's very good. We almost killed each other that day. All I wanted was a capture to fake the death." I swore I saw the muscle in Matthias's jaw move. But he still stayed silent, looking straight ahead, pretending I wasn't there.

"I spoke to Ian after that, and we determined that there was no way that I was going to be able to take him. He would have to come willingly. He would have to try and protect me. I don't know why, but Ian was very keen on keeping him alive and bringing him in."

It was Rafe who stood this time. "I'll bet he was. But he's not going to fucking get him. What the fuck was Ian thinking? He's basically started an all-out war."

Noah rolled his shoulders. "Oh, I certainly am not going to take her word for it. We'll talk to Ian. Then, if everything checks out, we'll deal with the ramifications." He turned his attention back to me. "What was Ian going to do with Matthias?"

"Do with him? Save his life, right? That's why I was here… to get him out safely, and keep him from hurting me and anyone else, and to get him somewhere safe. The Family is coming for him. One way or the other, they're going to get him."

Noah shook his head. "You don't know *this* family. Matthias isn't going anywhere, and we can take care of our own."

"Look, I believe you, but you don't know how violent they are. They will stop at nothing. Look, his life depends—"

Noah shook his head. "Stop. Stop talking. Now! You need to leave. I'm going to make that call to Ian. The only reason I'm not putting a detail on you is you wouldn't know Ian's code name if you weren't a member of ORUS. I'm going to send you home to your boss and he can handle you how he sees fit."

"You don't understand. Matthias is in danger. Look, the last time I spoke to the Family, they were insistent that I give them proof of death, which obviously I haven't. And then they told me that they would hurt Sabine if I couldn't deliver. They made it clear that they could get to Matthias. They said I was to tell him 'From the shadows comes the sun.'"

Rafe shoved his hands in his pockets. "What the fuck does that mean?"

"I have no fucking idea," said Noah.

"I don't know either," I said. "But the fact that Father got on the phone and told me to repeat that phrase, it must mean something. I don't know how much you know, or how much Matthias has told you, but we were both in the Family. As kids we knew each other. We had different names, of course. Matthias was my protector." I turned deliberately to look at him, but he still wouldn't meet my gaze. When I turned back to Noah and Rafe, they both scowled at me.

"Hell of a way to treat your old friend," Rafe said.

"Look, I know. I know I messed this up, but the last thing I want is for anything to happen to Matthias. Matthias, does that phrase mean anything to you?"

He didn't answer me. It was as if I weren't there.

Noah glanced between me and Matthias. "Kid, look, I'm going to get her out of here. You, me, and Rafe are going to talk, okay?" Still, there was no response.

I wanted to reach out and touch him. Reassure him in some way to let him know that I still cared about him. That part wasn't fake. That part wasn't the lie.

I knew I'd messed this up. I'd ruined everything. And now, Matthias was paying for it, and Sabine would too, with her life.

Rafe

I watched Matthias carefully. There was something wrong with the kid; I could see it. His eyes were cold, dead, flat. Not anything like what I'd been seeing lately.

Of late, I had started to see signs that maybe Noah was right. That maybe, just maybe, the kid was reachable, but not anymore.

Gemma was refusing to leave. She was trying to explain away that she could betray Matthias and betray them all. And then, of course, they had Ian to deal with.

Noah was going to kill him now. It was almost certain. And considering Ian had saved Noah, just like Andromeda had saved Gemma, that was going to be difficult and a problem. While Noah dealt with the girl, I turned to Matthias. "Listen kid, I know it feels like dirt right now, but this will straighten out. No one knows better than me that you can't look to your past to define you. You can't trust people from your past. Sometimes your past can be used against you. Do you understand what I'm saying?"

The kid still didn't respond. He was just staring that vacant and dead stare. Should we go ahead and call Dr. Breckner? Because this was terrifying.

And then it happened. In one split second, I took my eye off the ball. When I glanced at Noah, I said, "Listen, maybe you just give Matthias an eye—"

I never did finish what I was saying because pandemonium hit. In a sliver of a hair of a second, Matthias lunged after Gemma.

For the last ten minutes, the kid hadn't moved, hadn't budged, and hadn't blinked. And then all of a sudden, he craned his neck and his gaze pinned on Gemma. Then he was out of that chair and lunging for her.

Motherfucker!

Noah and I sprang into action. No one went around the table. I didn't have time to play that shit. I just went right over it. I tried to pull Matthias off of Gemma, but Gemma was no delicate flower and she was fighting back. Even though Matthias had his hands on her neck and was squeezing, Gemma had managed to wedge an arm between them.

But the kid was still on top of her with intent to do her harm. I tried to force an arm under Matthias's body and then twirled to disconnect his hold. But it didn't work. Matthias had braced himself.

Oh shit. He's going to fucking kill her.

Gemma choked and fought against him, and finally, she managed to bring one arm down sharply, but nothing happened. Then she did a simple pluck motion with her fingertips against the fleshy part of his thumbs. He released her and she dragged in sharp breaths.

Matthias loosened his hold, but he jerked back with an elbow then went straight for my nose.

When it connected, I howled and stumbled backwards.

By that time, Noah had reached him, taken Gemma and shoved her behind him. But Gemma wasn't going down easily. Even though she was still choking, she was fighting to stay on her feet and come after Matthias. She kept calling to him. "Matthias, it's me. It's me Gemma. Please, stop."

Yeah lady, like that's going to work. You just tripped his homicidal killer switch.

They needed to summon some sort of solution and quickly before Matthias killed them all.

Noah might love the kid, but he still wouldn't hesitate to take all actions to put him down.

The punches and kicks I took made me grind my teeth, but then Noah was back on his feet, ready to fight more. I kept taking the supposedly easy shots: kidneys; side; right under the ribs; gut. The face was more difficult to avoid, but for that, Matthias just took it on his chin like a champ. Jesus Christ, the kid could have been a boxer.

Matthias managed to grab Noah and knock his head against the wall. That rang Noah's bell for sure. And then Matthias was back to jumping on Gemma. This time though, he couldn't get a good hold because she kicked and put some good distance between them, jumped back, and then her hands were up, ready to go.

For every move, there was an equal and an opposite move. Her hands were flying. She took one of his hits to her right ribs. And that one unsettled her, I could tell. Shit, she probably had a bone broken or something. But

Matthias was going after her hard. The problem was this wasn't an angry attack. He had that dead look on his face like he was playing a video game. He couldn't even see her.

Things didn't get really hairy until Matthias picked up Gemma against the glass wall and shoved, repeating the action until her head rolled forward and the glass behind her broke. *Holy Mother of God!*

She'd unleashed the monster, and now it was ready to play.

———

Matthias

ANGER.

Hate.

Fear.

So much fear.

I didn't even know what I was fighting. Why I was fighting. What was so important that I had to kill these people? For a brief moment, I glanced down at Gemma's moaning, limp body, and a part of me wanted to reach out to her, to dust off the glass and tend to her cuts and hold her.

No, it wasn't like that. It was more.

I shook my head, trying to dislodge the memories of her taste, her touch, her smell.

I turned around. Rafe was coming for me, trying to stop me. Trying to kill me? I glanced back down at her and knew what I had to do. The best defense against someone like Rafe was offense. Before Rafe could get close, I lunged. I delivered one upper cut. Rafe's head snapped back and he cursed loudly.

Noah was scrambling forward. But Noah was also the kind that talked to me. "Listen, kid, you don't want to do this. You don't want to go there. We're family, remember?"

"I have no family."

Noah frowned. "Fair enough, if that's what you want to believe. But I think of you as family. You're like that little brother I never had. I can take care of you. I helped you."

"You called that help? I'm a fucking killer. I'm a murderer."

I threw a punch. Noah deftly sidestepped it and adjusted his stance.

I made the same adjustments to my body. Noah had gone from a Krav Maga stance with his hands up, back foot slightly raised, ready to pounce and move forward to a more jujitsu stance with a lower center of gravity. Like he wanted to tackle me and take me to the ground for a good grapple.

I wasn't going to be taken unaware. Noah had training, so right now, he knew everything I knew. The outlier was Rafe.

Rafe prowled around us, knowing that Noah needed to deliver a message, but also likely not wanting to hurt either one of us.

I watched Rafe warily. I remembered how the guy had almost killed me.

Noah's gaze shifted ever so briefly to the door, and that was it. I was on him like flies on shit. With one elbow to the temple, Noah's body was going down, and I jumped on him, raining punches on his face even as Noah tried haphazardly to stop them.

I was able to get a good four hits or so before Rafe launched at me, knocking me off his friend.

But not this time. I had pure rage, hatred, and fear on my side. Even though Rafe was better at blocking my punches, he didn't have the leverage right now. I knocked him over, delivering whatever would land: punches, elbows, a head-butt, I even pushed myself up briefly, getting a little height on my body before dropping back down with my knee on Rafe's gut.

Rafe wheezed, and out of the corner of my eye, I saw Noah was snapping out of it and was starting to move.

Motherfucker. I'd be up in a minute. But I knew that

Rafe was a larger danger. Noah, at least, didn't *want* to hurt me. There was always a part of Rafe that wanted to hurt all of us. On the other side of the room lay Gemma. She was starting to come to, as well. Her hands were drifting over glass as she tried to find purchase. I would have to go. They weren't going to let me kill her.

Do you want to kill her? No, I didn't, but I couldn't seem to stop myself.

When I had my hands around Rafe's neck, I wedged a knee on one of his arms. That meant Rafe couldn't push me off. He wheezed as he clawed with his hands, but I was not letting go. When Noah finally pushed himself to standing and ran over to us, I had to divert my attention, because in that moment my one objective was to kill Rafe and then get to Gemma and kill her. Finish the job.

But Noah wasn't having that. He dragged me backward, kicking and screaming.

"Damn it, Matthias, enough. I don't know what the fuck is going on with you, but if you cannot get it together, I will put you down."

And that was the problem with Noah. My mentor, my friend, would always choose to talk first before fighting. I was a different breed of animal altogether.

The blade was easy to reach, always at my fingertips. At any given time, I always had at least three or four of them. I liked knives. They were easy to conceal. And they were deadly.

I slid the knife from its sheath at the back of my belt and swiped in a wide arch going from right to left.

Noah hissed and then cursed, his hand going over his stomach and then pulling away as he stared at the blood. "Matthias, what have you done?"

I saw my mentor start to wobble and then fall. The problem was that little impromptu fight session had drawn attention. Lucia was running toward the conference room.

I wondered if I'd make it to Gemma. I had to kill her. Those were my orders. Would I have the time? Because right behind Lucia was Diana. And she was armed. Diana carried that gun around everywhere. The woman was one hell of a shot.

I didn't want to, but after careful assessment, I knew I had to leave her. I would come back for her though.

I had to go, but it was Noah who stopped me, reaching for me, still on his knees, still trying to plant a foot, to get back up.

"Matthias, you don't have to do this."

I stared down at the man who had been like a second father to me in some ways. "Yes, I do. You all have to die." And then I plunged my knife into Noah's shoulder.

It was time to go.

———

THANK YOU for reading the first book of the SIN duet. The next book, *Sinful*, releases on 6/19/18. PREORDER NOW at malonesquared.com/sin

While you're waiting, catch up on Jonas and JJ's story, FORCE! Keep reading for an excerpt.

EXCERPT OF FORCE

For years I've existed on the edge of the dark, protecting innocents who can't protect themselves. Until... her. Jessica JJ Jones. The bane of my existence. A bright light in the dark. The crack in my armor. A loud, argumentative beautiful crack in my armor.

But first, there's a more immediate concern. JJ is running

scared. And to protect her I might have to break the vow I made years ago.

———

Excerpt of Force © August 2017 M. Malone and Nana Malone

Jessica Jones closed her eyes, exhausted. Day after draining day of pulling double duty while her bestie and partner in crime was on maternity leave was starting to take its toll. Like hell was she going to start complaining, though. If anyone deserved happiness, it was Lucia. Her best friend had been to hell and back and deserved the time off.

JJ could deal. After all Lucia would do it for her. Besides, JJ wasn't letting a prima donna fashion designer run her into the ground and call uncle. She'd rather burn her Jimmy Choos first. She could handle anything their boss Adriana could dish out.

It felt like she'd only shut her eyes for mere seconds before she frowned in her sleep.

Something was wrong. *Very* wrong.

When she peeled her eyes open again, she was in hell.

"Oh my god," she screamed.

But that scream was her first mistake. It meant emptying out her lungs, which meant she needed to breathe... and that meant lungs full of smoke.

It was so hot her hair plastered against her head and her sheets clung to her naked breasts from sweat. Yeah, she slept topless, so what? It had been so hot lately.

Frantic, she looked around the room trying to find the source of heat. It was so dark she couldn't see anything. But she could feel the smoke all around her, cloying and thick, wrapping around her and constricting her lungs.

"Don't panic." The sound of her own voice out loud scared her out of her frozen state. *Fear immobilizes. Anger motivates.* That's right, get pissed off!

If there was anything JJ was good at, it was being hot tempered. What the fuck was smoke doing in her room anyway? She'd just had a goddamned blowout. She needed to charge that color and cut to whatever or whoever was the source of this fire.

Move your ass girly.

She had to move because she was *not* dying in this room. She did not survive her past to die like this. Fuck that noise. Besides, if she died like this, Lucia would resurrect her ass and kill her all over again. After Lucia had survived being stalked and almost killed, JJ had a new appreciation for the meaning of life.

She swung her legs over the side of the bed, letting out a sigh of relief when her toes met the carpet. Now that her eyes had adjusted to the dark somewhat, she could see the faint hint of an orange glow from down the hall. Which meant the fire hadn't reached her room... yet.

But the bedroom door stood open to the hall, which was probably why she could already smell the smoke.

It was weird that the door was open. She always closed the door before going to sleep. It was one of the things Lucia's husband had drilled into her. Noah owned a security company, and his overprotectiveness toward Lucia had spilled over onto JJ. Now she always had one of the annoying, albeit sexy, guys who worked for him trailing her to and from work, and her apartment had been subjected to a thorough security 'review' by Noah's resident IT wizard. Matthias had deemed her place 'merely acceptable.'

JJ was pretty sure they'd have asked her to move if they hadn't known from experience that she didn't take suggestions well. The last thing she needed was some man trying to tell her what to do. Maybe Lucia was okay with that, but she wasn't interested. JJ knew from experience that she didn't want any man having control over her life. Never again. That alpha-asshole shit didn't work for her, so they could shove their over protectiveness where the sun didn't shine.

With a quick glance at the open door, she realized it was actually lucky she'd left it open, otherwise she might not have woken up until the flames were closer. What the hell had woken her? *You can think through that shit after you're safe.* Yeah, good point. She grabbed up her comforter and wrapped herself in the thick fabric, bringing it up over her head as she stepped into a pair of slippers.

How far to the door? The window might be an option if the fire escape hadn't been welded over some years ago. She looked up and then squinted in the darkness. And then she saw the shadow in the hall. The man-sized shadow.

Fuck me. She opened her mouth to scream then reached into her bedside drawer for the nearest weapon she could find. She'd been aiming for the retractable baton she kept in the top drawer. But instead she'd come up with a gag gift from a bachelorette party a couple of years ago. A giant purple vibrator.

What are you gonna do with that? Fuck him to death? Well that was a thought.

"Who the hell are you? And what the fuck are you doing in my apartment?"

He stepped forward slightly, his body still half-hidden outside the door, and JJ raised her makeshift weapon.

"I'm here for you, Jessica. I'm always here for you."

JJ clutched the blanket closer, and her fingers curled around the vibrator as his voice washed over her. The low tone of his words sliced through her veins. That voice. It had been so long since she'd heard that voice. She'd hoped to never hear it again, except in her nightmares.

"How did you find me?"

His chuckle was almost as terrifying as the words that followed. "I never lost you."

JJ screamed and backed up so fast that she stumbled and fell on the bed. The comforter tangled around her and she fought against it, certain the next touch she'd feel would be the last.

Strong hands wrapped around her flailing arms.

"Damn it, you crazy woman, I'm trying to help you!"

It took a few seconds before she recognized the voice, her terror distorting it into the one she feared most. When she finally spoke, her voice was tiny.

"Jonas? Is that you?"

The comforter was pulled back away from her eyes,

and Jonas's handsome face appeared. Jonas Castillo worked for Noah's security company and was a regular fixture in her life. He was routinely assigned to protect Lucia, and by default JJ, during the workweek. She took great pleasure in giving him hell, and he was usually cursing her name or bickering with her.

"Yes, of course it's me."

Before she could question what he was doing there, she felt herself being lifted. She clutched his shoulders automatically, disoriented after her fall. Now she wasn't sure if that had actually happened. Had she been dreaming? It was so hard to tell.

"Jonas, did you see anyone else in the apartment?"

"Like who? Don't you live alone?"

Was that jealousy in his voice? Even under these circumstances, JJ couldn't resist the urge to screw with him a little.

"Actually I don't. We can't leave without my favorite guy."

"Who? And if you have a boyfriend, where is he? Some help he is during an emergency."

"Well, Fluffy has never been much help during emergencies, but he blows the best wet kisses."

Jonas didn't pause. "I'll come back for your dog, I promise. But I have to get you to safety."

It must have been the smoke affecting her brain,

because at first JJ didn't realize what he'd said. It wasn't until they were at the front door that she understood he meant to leave.

"No! I have to get Fluffy!" JJ swatted at his massive chest. She must have surprised him because his arms loosened around her legs, giving her the room she needed to jump down.

"Damn it, JJ! This is serious. We don't have time to stop."

"It'll just take a second." JJ raced back to the guest bedroom and grabbed Fluffy, covering him with the comforter as she ran.

Jonas picked her up as soon as she hit the hallway and ran for the front door. They passed a crew of fire-fighters in the corridor outside her apartment. The smoke was thicker out here, so JJ buried her face in Jonas's shoulder, making sure to keep Fluffy covered too.

When they got outside, Jonas set them down carefully on the grass, safely away from the building. An EMT approached, and Jonas pointed at JJ. She was going to protest, but dissolved into a coughing fit as soon as she opened her mouth. The young man frowned and knelt on the grass next to her. Then his eyes widened when her comforter slipped and she almost flashed an entire boob at him.

"Hey, eyes up, kid." Jonas glared at him before yanking his shirt off. He put it over JJ's head, and she maneuvered carefully to get her arms in without dropping the comforter completely. If she hadn't felt so crappy, she'd have told him exactly where he could shove it. She didn't need anyone speaking for her.

Just to annoy him, she gave the EMT a bright smile that had the young man blushing furiously. Jonas scowled at both of them.

After a flurry of activity, blood pressure cuffs, and oxygen, they finally left her alone. That's when Jonas got a good look at her again. Her *and* Fluffy.

"A fish? You risked your life to save a fucking fish?"

JJ scooped up Fluffy's bowl protectively. "Fluffy is not just a fish. He's a Japanese fighting fish. A total badass."

Jonas looked like he wanted to strangle her. Normally that was exactly the effect she was going for, but strangely, it wasn't as satisfying as usual.

"Thank you, Jonas. For coming in after me."

He looked as shocked as she felt by her sudden gratitude.

"Of course. It's nothing. The fire department would have gotten to you soon. I just happened to get there first when Matthias said your alarms were triggered."

The talk of alarms brought back memories of the man she'd seen in the smoke. It had happened so fast, and she couldn't be sure what was real and what had been a dream.

"Did you see anyone in there?" At his confused look, JJ clarified, "In my apartment?"

Jonas knelt and looked her in the eye. "Was there someone in there with you, Jessica?"

It was all such a blur, and she didn't like the way he was looking at her. Noah's entire crew was extremely overprotective, so if she said the wrong thing, she'd end up on house arrest with Jonas as her jailor. Plus, it was likely it had all been a dream. Jonas had been in her apartment. He would have seen if anyone else was there. The man in the smoke was nothing more than a shadow from a past she'd rather forget.

"No, I meant in the building. I just want to make sure all my neighbors got out okay."

Jonas looked like he wanted to say something else, but Noah arrived just then with Lucia right behind him.

JJ accepted a hug from her friend, and that was when it really hit her.

"I guess I'm homeless now."

Noah's voice carried from behind Lucia. "You'll stay with us, of course."

JJ's eyes met Jonas's, and she knew he was thinking about her earlier question.

"It's for the best," Jonas said.

She glanced over at Lucia. "Free rent and a house full of hot men. Count me in."

Read FORCE now at malonesquared.com/force

ABOUT THE AUTHORS

NYT & USA Today Bestselling author **M. MALONE** lives in the Washington, D.C. metro area with her three favorite guys, her husband and their two sons. She holds a Master's degree in Business from a prestigious college that would no doubt be scandalized at how she's using her expensive education.

Independently published, her work has appeared on the New York Times and USA Today bestseller lists more than a dozen times. She's now a full-time writer and spends 99.8% of her time in her pajamas. **minxmalone.com**

USA Today Bestselling Author, **NANA MALONE**'s love of all things romance and adventure started with a tattered romantic suspense she borrowed from her cousin on a sultry summer afternoon in Ghana at a precocious thirteen. She's been in love with kick butt heroines ever since.

With her overactive imagination, and channeling her inner Buffy, it was only a matter a time before she started creating her own characters. Waiting for her chance at a job as a ninja assassin, Nana, meantime works out her drama, passion and sass with fictional characters every bit as sassy and kick butt as she thinks she is. **nanamaloneromance.net**